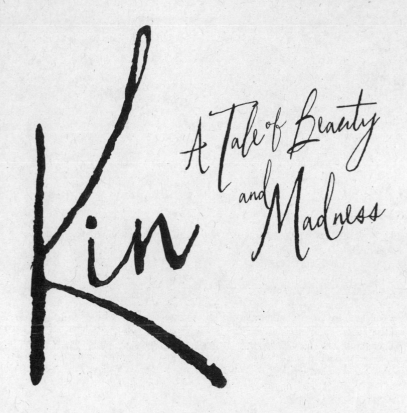

Kin

A Tale of Beauty and Madness

LILI ST. CROW

razOr
bill

An Imprint of Penguin Group (USA)

A division of Penguin Young Readers Group
Published by the Penguin Group
Penguin Group (USA) LLC
345 Hudson Street
New York, New York 10014

USA / Canada / UK / Ireland / Australia / New Zealand / India / South Africa / China
Penguin.com
A Penguin Random House Company

ISBN: 978-1-59514-621-2

Printed in the United States of America

1 3 5 7 9 10 8 6 4 2

FOR YOU

Kin

PROLOGUE:

SHORTCUTS

TWO DARK-HAIRED YOUNG MEN, LEANING ON EACH other as if drunk. One of them reels, retching and coughing, the other makes soft soothing noises. There is a faint gleam—something silver, plucked from the drunkard's pocket. He grabs for it, almost topples, and his helper speaks softly.

This is a small town, and the train is waiting. The two have twenty minutes before the train is resealed and plunges through the Waste, flora and fauna both Twisted from stagnant and wild Potential. Sometimes a train derails, other times, things attack the metal intrusion. So far, though, this journey has been uneventful.

There is an alley close to the station. Its shadowed mouth swallows both young men. The darkness is complete, except for a few faint gleams—silver, again. A swaying, a sharp arc of brilliance. A meaty, thudding sound.

When a young man boards the train later, he looks faintly

troubled. But he has plenty of time to reach his sleeper compartment, and is settled on a wide, comfortable seat folded down into a bed when the whistle blows, a high piercing demand. Layers of charm seal the train again, and anyone left behind for any reason has to stay in this small town. To leave anywhere, you must pay for a fresh ticket. And a new indemnity, in case the Waste eats the train.

Or worse.

Steam billows. Cinders fall, dirty snow, and the metal beast heaves forward.

Afterward, the station is deserted. The town slumbers, too small for its sleep to be troubled by the problems of cities—urban cores full of slopping-over Potential, a Waste of its own. There was always the small, remote chance that the Waste might move in, and swallow the town whole. The next train to come through could well encounter a wilderness, its walls shattered and its buildings jumbled, its inhabitants no longer draining off Potential to restore their surroundings to normality.

Around the station, unTwisted trees planted beside ruler-straight sidewalks rustle, their thin branches shaken by a hot wind from the Waste as a maggot-cheese moon rises higher in an uncaring sky.

The train's whistle, in the distance, is a lonely, mournful song.

PART I:

INTO THE WOODS

ONE

NEW HAVEN RECLINED UNDER THICK SUNSHINE AND fluffy cotton-wool clouds, isolated trees turning to autumn flames early this year. The rest were still that peculiar darkening green they wore right before dressing up for Dead Harvest.

Less than a week of freedom between the end of summer classes and the beginning of the last year at St. Juno's, which meant that if you wanted to have some fun you had to grab it with both hands. It was even better when you had friends to help with the grabbing and pulling.

Which sort of explained why Ruby de Varre was sitting cross-legged on her Semprena's still-warm bonnet, at the park on top of Haven Hill, completely alone. Summer was stuttering to a stop, so it was still warm in the sunshine, but here under a huge spreading oak tree that probably predated the Reeve there was an edge to the breeze. This tree hadn't started turning yet, still green and vital, the sound of its leaves rubbing against each other a snakescale whisper.

Cami and Ellie had both promised to meet her at Stellar's to get milkshakes before figuring out how best to waste this pretty nice day together. After fifteen with no sign of either she'd bailed, because who had time to wait around with so little summer left?

That just meant she was up here all alone, staring at New Haven spread out below the Hill like a fresh banquet in front of a glutton too stuffed to eat another bite. All that excitement, all that life pulsing under the ribbons of pavement, from the blighted core to the Moving Wall that separated city from Waste . . . and here she was, in jeans and a red tank top instead of school uniform but nobody to talk to. Nothing to *do*.

Maybe she could have stayed and waited.

Why bother, though? Ellie was always on about *Avery* this and *Avery* that, and talking about the scholarships lined up with the help of the Fletcher charm-clan. Her Potential had settled and her stepmother'd been shipped off to a kolkhoz, and that was just fine by Ruby on both counts, but every other word coming out of Ellie's mouth was about the boyfriend nowadays.

At least Cami didn't talk about Nico much, but she'd been even quieter than usual lately, something about etiquette among the Seven. The Families ruled New Haven but continually jostled each other, and there was some slight or another that required some diplomacy and extra gatherings. Of course, Cami as *la Vultusina* had to organize a few of them as neutral ground. So she was always looking off in the distance, probably worrying about caterers or how to keep Family members from drawing any blood.

Literally.

Ruby sighed, leaning back on her hands. The smell of hot earth, the tang of the trees beginning to turn, exhaust from engines throbbing all through New Haven, pollen, cut grass somewhere. If her nose had begun to tingle, she could follow it and find some fun.

There was just no fun to be scented today.

She couldn't even bask, because she'd parked in the shade, as usual. Cami didn't complain about sunshine, but why take chances, right? Now that Cami was . . . whatever she was, with Nico Vultusino finally stepping up and sharing his family's, well, *peculiarities* with her, she liked to keep out of the sun's eye. *I'm not going to c-combust,* she'd said, trying to explain it to Ruby. *It's just . . . uncomfortable.*

So parking in the shade made her more comfortable, and Ruby was in the habit of caring about things like that.

She squinted, and could barely see, in the hazy distance, the gray bulk of St. Juno's. Just yesterday she'd squeaked through the High Charm Calculus final, mostly thanks to Ell's patient tutelage and a healthy dose of luck. That caught her up after all the skipping; Mother Heloise had called all three of them into her office and told them to stay out of trouble in the upcoming year.

Last year of high school. Which meant the last year before she had to Take Responsibility. Oh, there was Ebermerle Charmcollege to attend, but a Woodsdowne girl had Duties when she turned eighteen. To the clan, to the kin, to the world. As Gran was always reminding her.

You could grow into anything, given enough time. It wasn't Gran's fault Ruby was lagging.

She sighed again, shaking her head, and hopped off the Semprena's glossy blackness. Her key ring jangled as she spun it around one finger, and she caught herself grimacing. Most of her summer wasted, and her two best friends standing her up. Fifteen minutes wasn't forever, but still. It was the principle of the thing, that was all.

No, it's not. It's the collaring.

The thought stopped her in her tracks. She stared up at the oak's whispering leaves. Her skin itched a little, all over. A few deep breaths and that deep persistent scratching faded.

Gran couldn't have meant it, could she? Collaring was for kin who couldn't control themselves, not for girls who didn't do what their grandmothers wanted. Right?

I should collar you, to save you from yourself. Gran's mouth a thin line, the disapproval emanating from her in waves. All because Ruby had wanted to dance out the door without doing the dishes, and moaned theatrically when Gran called it to her attention.

Well, maybe that wasn't quite it. She'd moaned, and stamped into the kitchen, and accidentally bumped a coffee mug into the sink. Where it shattered, and Gran maybe thought Ruby had done it deliberately?

You cannot control yourself!

It wasn't fair. She had *plenty* of control. To prove it, Ruby put her hand out into the sunlight, past the dappled leafshade. Concentration made a knot behind her forehead, and the smells around her became sharper, more vivid, bursting in through her nose and painting pictures.

The rippling under her skin intensified. Like little mice, *mus*, the root word for *muscles*. A stippling, and a few scattered, fine golden-rust hairs sticking up.

Not quite painful, more like a stinging sunburn, the spots of fluid moving shade farther up her forearm a shielding coolness, twitching against her nerves.

Her nails lengthened, translucent tips hardening. Wicked-sharp, her wrist bulging oddly on one side as her hand became something . . . different.

Ruby exhaled, sharply, and forced it down. There were prickles of sweat along her lower back and under her arms, despite the breeze. Easy-peasy. Nothing to it.

She wasn't even *angry*. Well, maybe a little, but that—

The cramps hit, right below her ribs. Ruby doubled over, denying the dry-heaving, shoving the sensation away. It was dangerous to shift partway, because everything in you would cry out for release.

Stray curls fell in front of her face, their red-gold burnished by more sunshine, because she'd stepped out in the full flood of it. The stinging all over her drove her into a crouch, and her palms met warm pavement with a jolt. It was work to tip her face up, her closed eyes filling with rubescent glow, lips skinned back from teeth. Finally, breath coming fast and hard, she levered herself back up and examined her hands.

Tanned, and human. She was Woodsdowne rootfamily, she was kin, and she was in control. Gran couldn't mean what she'd said about collaring Ruby to calm her down.

Except Gran rarely said things she didn't mean. *Rarely* was something of an understatement. It was more like, well, *never*.

Ruby swore, softly, and picked up her keys. There was nothing to do and nowhere sounded interesting.

Might as well go home.

"I'm *heeeeere!*" The door to the garage banged shut, and Ruby prance-galloped through the utility room as if she was six again. She danced into the living room, the tapestry with a charmer's sun-and-moon whispering as its threads shifted, the sun's broad smile turned knowing and friendly. Every chair and couch was overstuffed, and the place would have looked cluttered if not for Gran's ruthless organization. Everything had a place, and there were boxes and baskets and dishes to hold *everything*. Gran did her active charming in a workroom off her downtown office, but she charmed at home, too. So there were the sealed bottles of charmahol and sylph-ether in the utility room, and jars containing small things—feathers, bones, brass discs, other tiny items that could hold a charge of Potential or finished charm.

Everything was jewel toned, but the shades were dark and restful. Royal blue, deep hunter green, accents of gold and thin threads of crimson, everything placed just-so.

Gran was in front of the fireplace, just straightening and brushing her hands as if to rid them of noxious dust. Crackling Potential limned her—the kin didn't often throw high-powered charmers, but she was one of them. Oh, sure, every kin *could* charm a little, especially since the Reeve, but not like Gran. She could probably even set Ellie back on her heels, and Ell was a prodigy.

For a moment Gran's gray eyes glowed with their own internal light, and her parchment hair, braided and pinned with ruthless precision, caught the radiance of the tall bronze lamps with their rice-paper shades. Afternoon sun pouring through the wide front windows almost seemed to go *through* her, despite the cheerful colors of her dragon-patterned housedress.

Edalie de Varre, who controlled import and export through the Waste outside New Haven, wrinkled her aristocratic nose slightly as Ruby came to a skidding halt before her and dropped a tolerable curtsy.

"Good afternoon, Granmere." Cheerfulness dripped from

every syllable, the camouflage old and comfortable as a pair of worn trainers. "Charming as always, I see." The air around them both rippled with Potential, waves Ruby could almost-see, the smells of hay and fur and food comforting and familiar. There was beef under a defrost-charm in the kitchen, one corner of the High Charm Calc equation unknotted so the temperature would equalize swiftly, shaking off ice and keeping the meat safe. Maybe Gran planned stew or stir-fry tonight.

Gran's mouth twitched. On another person, it would have been a fleeting expression, too small to be seen, but on her it was loud as a shout. Ruby, relieved at this sign of forgiveness, threw her arms around the older woman and hugged—gently. Gran wasn't fragile, by *any* stretch of the imagination . . . but still.

Edalie patted Ruby's tangled hair. "Good afternoon, child. I was experimenting with live flame and a Beaudrell's charm."

"Ellie would know if that's a good thing or not." Ruby shut her eyes for a moment, breathing in safety and comfort. There was a black ribbon of burning, the thread stitching together every other scent that made up *home*. That was funny; a Beaudrell's charm was supposed to be odorless.

"You should know too." Gran didn't sound precisely disappointed, but it was close.

I do know. It's not a good idea, but if you're an active and experienced charmer, you can escape having it blow up and singe your eyebrows. "How am I going to be a disappointment to the entire clan if I know things like that?" The instant it was out of her mouth she regretted it, but said was said.

Gran's hand merely paused before continuing. "Is that your goal?"

Don't be ridiculous. "Of course not." *I just don't see how it's not going to happen.* "Beaudrell's Charms can be used to control open flame, but the secret of precisely how died with Beaudrell himself." She made it into a singsong, letting the history lesson jump out hopscotch-quick. "Anton Beaudrell, died in '56, famous for his control of fire and the advances he made in preservation charms. Married into the Creighton charmclan of Manahat Province, it was also whispered he had a touch of the fey in his veins—"

"Untrue. I met the man once, and was not impressed. He was no Child of Danu." Gran's arms loosened, and though Ruby wanted to hold on, she knew better.

So she loosened up, and made sure she was smiling. "You've met *everyone.*"

Gran stepped carefully away. "Living does tend to bring the world to one's door."

"I thought it was 'travel makes you meet interesting people.'"

"I dislike travel."

"You don't like driving long distances, and you hate trains."

A pained expression flitted across Gran's familiar face. Were the wrinkles getting deeper, or was Ruby just looking more closely now? "We're meeting a train tomorrow."

"Really? A business contact, or what?"

"Kin, my child. It's time."

Huh. "For what?"

"For you to see him again."

Kin. Not anyone interesting. She'd planned tonight to maybe see one of her regular boytoys before the moonrunning anyway. *Toy* was the only word that applied, since a Woodsdowne girl couldn't afford to go Too Far. Besides, they were all so weak-smelling. Easily roped in, and just as easily discarded.

Still, she feigned some interest. "Who?"

Maybe she'd see Brett; things hadn't heated up to their inevitable conclusion with *him* yet. Which meant him wanting to go further than making out, or thinking he could pressure her into it.

There was only once she'd been tempted to go Too Far, and it hadn't been with a mere-human. That one hot fullmoon night, strawberries and the musk of a kinboy, Thorne's fingertips, dyed with strawberry juice, feathering around the outside of her lips. Maybe she would have let him do what he wanted if they hadn't been interrupted by Hunter's approaching footsteps.

It was probably for the best. The two of them were always at each other in that way only boys who had grown up together could manage, with the added spice of kinstrength and claws.

Her grandmother made a small, dismissive sound. "A root-family boy from Grimtree clan. He's arriving tomorrow on the seven o'clock from up-province."

For a few moments it didn't make sense. The meaning of the words arrived, thunder after lightning, and Ruby almost rocked back on her heels. "I'm not even out of high school yet!"

"You wouldn't marry him right away." Gran apparently considered that to be the final word, and turned toward the kitchen. "Besides, you may not find him pleasing."

"I don't find *any* of this pleasing. It's medieval, to parade me in front of—"

"Oh, no. In those days, the males would have fought to submission or death to mate a kingirl, even if she evinced no interest. Times have changed."

Great. You sound like Oncle Efraim. "Is that supposed to be comforting? Jeez, Gran."

"His name is Conrad. Surely you remember?"

Conrad, from the Grimtree. It rang a bell. She'd been told the story a million times, how she'd whacked him on the head with a stuffed rabbit when he'd announced she was pretty. "I was *three.*"

"I knew you would recall it." Mithrus Christ, Gran sounded *pleased.* Before she vanished into the kitchen, she tossed one more little tidbit over her shoulder. "Also, your friend Cami called. She sounded quite worried, and hoped you were all right. I thought you were meeting her?"

"She didn't show up," Ruby managed, through numb lips. Of course Gran would think Ruby had lied about where she was going.

15

Wild kingirls sometimes did.

A guest from out of town meant that she'd have to give up almost her entire week to showing him around, acting like she was interested but not *too* interested, and pretending to be a little downcast when he left. With Gran watching every moment, making decisions. *It's for your own good, child.*

It always was. Tonight was moonrunning, too, and everyone would be asking her questions unless she avoided them. That avoidance would be judged and weighed, too, because *kin* meant *together.* Even solitaries craved the company of their own when the Moon rose full.

So much for the last week of summer. Ruby sighed, groaned theatrically one more time, and stamped for the stairs.

TWO

AN HOUR LATER, A CHARMBELL TINKLED SWEETLY, and Ruby, furiously working at a wad of choco beechgum, whipped the front door open to find her best friends on the step, the green tangle of the garden under thick gold sunlight behind them.

"*There* you are!" Cami looked a little pale, but maybe it was just the deep voracious blue of her eyes. She even smelled worried, a tang of bright lemon over a deeper well of ancient spice and healthy young girl. "We w-waited for an hour!"

Which was worse, to admit she'd only hung around fifteen minutes, or to let them think she'd blown them off? It was one of those unanswerable questions, like where the Reeve started or whether lightcharms worked more like particles or waves. "I thought you'd forgotten, so I left."

"Got caught in traffic." Ellie, her wavy platinum hair pulled back, tipped her sunglasses down. It was kind of a shock to see her in jeans without holes and a decent pair of boots, a luckcharm bracelet tinkling sweetly on one wrist. She wasn't as pale as Cami, and she'd put on a little weight, thank Mithrus. She'd been scary-thin when summer classes started, and scary-starey-eyed as well. "You okay?"

They depended on her to be the perfectly unreliable one, *quelle ironique.* "Come on in. Sorry, I thought you'd bailed to spend time with the boys. Or, you know, study or something."

"Why would . . ." Cami halted midway, stepping nervously over the threshold. Normally Ruby would have assumed the stutter was giving her some trouble, because she never used to be able to get a whole word out without trying a couple times. Ever since she'd disappeared last winter, kidnapped by a nightmare below New Haven, and been rescued, speaking had been easier. She was the closest thing to a sanity-anchor Nico Vultusino had, which was great—that boy *needed* something to put his brakes on, and Cami had quietly but definitely been moderating him even more lately.

Then there was Ellie, who glided into the front hall like she was on rails. Enough Potential to light up the city, a mad talent for charming, her *real* parents dead and her stepmother half-Twisted and shipped out into the Waste to a kolkhoz, good riddance and goodnight. Except Ell had disappeared for a while too, hanging out with some fey thing living near St. Juno's, and *that* hadn't ended well.

At least they were both still alive. A bit wide-eyed and twitchy, but alive.

Kin

It was a change to be considered the most drama-free of the three of them, and one Ruby wasn't quite sure she liked. Still, if she was going to start being responsible, better get used to it, right?

"I'm sorry." The words felt a little weird. There never used to be anything to apologize for, really.

Or had there, and she just hadn't noticed? Lately, she'd been asking herself that a lot.

"No problem." Ellie swept the door closed. "What do you want to do? If Avery drives we could even make a club tonight. You know, a grown-up place."

For what value of grown-up, if they'll let us in through the door? Still, the idea was powerfully attracting. "He can go out after curfew now?"

A shrug, but Ellie's eyes were dancing. "He's got the permit."

Which means we'd have to take him. "That would have done us some good a few weeks ago."

Ellie, ever the overachiever, looked a little horrified. "We were in *school* then."

Because Cami lost a ton of class time during the winter, and then you disappeared and we skipped everything to go around looking for you too. "Oh yeah. That means no fun, ever. Forgot about that."

Well, it had sounded funny in her head, but neither of them laughed.

Uncomfortable silence filled the hall to bursting, sloshing against the walls. Gran's cottage was in the heart of Woodsdowne, prime property, but it was small. You could tell she'd never expected to have company in here, much less the baby of a kingirl who wasn't ever spoken about.

Sometimes Ruby wondered about her mother. It would have been nice to know something more than the handful of whispers she'd managed to gather around the edges.

Whispers like *she was so beautiful, and Wild too.*

Really Wild, not just halfway there like Ruby. Maybe that was the trouble; she was watered-down instead of the real deal. If she was *really* Wild, she probably wouldn't have cared what Gran thought. Or maybe Gran would respect that, the way she respected Cami's quiet strength or Ellie's smarts.

Gran never spoke about Ruby's parents, except to once remark that Ruby looked like her mother, and confirm that her mother's mate was outclan. So she didn't have to worry about mingling with the closer branchkin.

Marrying too close wasn't good for the kin.

"You're angry." Cami folded her arms. Even on the hottest days she generally wore long sleeves, even though her scars had vanished.

A habit that old was hard to break.

"I am *not.*" To prove it, she folded her arms too, and took a deep breath. Gran could probably hear every word, no matter where in the house she was.

"W-we didn't *mean* to be late." A small vertical line had developed between Cami's perfect coal-arc eyebrows, and Ruby was abruptly conscious of her own wildly curling, uncombed hair, bare feet, chipped nail polish. Cami always looked so damn put-together. "What's wrong?"

She would be the one to notice any little thing, too. Since she didn't talk much, it was easy to be surprised when she made an observation.

Oh, nothing. I'm just probably going to be married off or collared because Gran thinks I'm too Wild. After expecting me to be Wild enough to qualify as rootfamily for years. When really I'm not Wild enough, and not sub enough to be calm and collected. Stuck in between. No big deal. She dredged up a smile, searching for her old familiar *I-couldn't-give-a-damn* voice. It came, like it always did, an old reliable friend. "Not a thing, sweets. I just can't go out tonight. Clan stuff."

Cami's face fell perceptibly, and Ellie's eyes darkened a shade or two. But Ell, as usual, immediately shifted to solve-the-problem mode. "Well, let's go have some fun now. I'll drive. And we can figure out what we're doing each day this week before school starts and write it down."

It's just so like you to plan out everything. "Houseguest."

"What?" Sudden changes in direction always threw Ell off, especially when she was arranging things.

Ruby felt a little guilty, but only a little. Disrupting the planning mode had a charm all its own. "We're getting a visitor, tomorrow. Some guy Gran might marry me off to once I'm out of charmcollege."

The announcement had its intended effect. Both of them looked thunderstruck. The line between Cami's eyebrows went away, and her cherry-glossed lips parted a little, as if she was working on a knotty High Charm Calc problem. Ellie actually rocked back on her heels—the boots were PaxGrecas, and well worn, so they still said *money* but they did it in a couth whisper.

"It's about time," Ruby continued, hoping Gran was listening. "Gotta be more responsible, right? Last year of high school and all. So anyway. Where are we going?"

In the end, they couldn't decide where to go, so they flopped down on the living-room couches, the conversation turning in lazy circles as the tapestry's threads made that maddening little sound. There was a sort of perverse pleasure to be had in shrugging and saying, "I don't know, it'll depend on the visitor" when Ellie tried to time out the next week in precise increments. Cami watched both of them, her expression a mix of concentration and worry, just as it had always been.

It was almost a relief when Ellie sighed and glanced at the clock. "I'm due home for dinner soon. Ruby, is there any time at *all* that we can hang out before school starts?"

Well, wasn't that guilt-inducing. "I'll try. I just . . . you know, Gran wants me to do things."

"I know." Ellie rose in one fluid motion, her Potential a brief, sparkling arc for a moment as the atmosphere of another charmer's cottage changed around her.

Cami followed suit, more slowly. "I'll have a c-car tomorrow." She spaced the words out carefully, brushing back a few glossy strands of raven hair. "Nico ordered it special from over-Waste. A Spyder. So whenever you call, I can come."

"Well hot *damn*. That's great news." There was a funny little tickle in Ruby's chest. She and Ellie wouldn't need rides home from Juno anymore, being Year 12s and able to drive on their own. That had been Rube's job for *forever*. "What color?"

"Sort of cream, I guess. He tells me Spyders are p-pretty safe."

"Safe?" Ellie's eyebrows nested in her hairline. "I guess, if you overlook that made-of-charmfiber-and-goes-like-the-wind thing. Hey, when you get it, can Ave look at the engine?"

The urge to roll her eyes was *immense*. It was Boy Mentionitis in a big way—every other sentence was about Avery. Ell hadn't even noticed boys *existed* before, so it was probably a natural stage in her dating evolution. Even an idiot could tell Ave was serious about her, which was nice to see. It meant one more person keeping her out of trouble.

"I guess." Cami crossed her arms as if she was cold, rubbing at them through her sleeves. "Maybe I can even find out how an engine works. Fun."

"You press the accelerator and it *goes*." Ruby bounced up from the couch. "What more do you need to know?"

"How to keep it going, how to brake, how to—"

"I'm not *stupid*, Ell. It was a joke."

More uncomfortable silence. Finally Cami cleared her throat, a small soft sound. "Today's not a good day. I'll call you both d-day after t-tomorrow. And we are *going* to hang out." Polite but very definite, with her blue eyes level and serious, she suddenly looked less like a little girl playing dress-up and more, well, adult.

It happened to everyone sooner or later.

"Yes ma'am." Ruby sketched her a cheerful salute, but her heart had fallen right into her guts with a gurgling splash. "I'll even wear heels."

"We could go shopping." From Ellie, that was a peace of-fering—her stepmother had worked in couture, and going into boutiques and ateliers turned Ell an interesting shade of pale sometimes. "Anywhere you want."

It shouldn't have stung, but it sounded like offering a bratty five-year-old a treat. Ruby pushed her temper down with an almost-physical effort. "I'll make a list."

It wasn't until they were safely out of the driveway—the sun blazing down despite fat-bellied shadows drifting over the city from fleecy clouds, gilding the primer-splotched Del Toro Ell borrowed from Avery Fletcher whenever she felt like it—

that Ruby's shoulders unknotted. She'd played the holy terror for them again, and also gave Gran a few indications of responsibility.

If she could just keep this balancing act up, everything would be easy.

THREE

Woodsdowne Park, a green beating chamber in New Haven's slow ponderous heart, always filled slowly with summer dusk. Here the trees hadn't started to turn yet, not even a few, and she wouldn't have put it past them to petition Gran for permission before they started to paint themselves. Summer lingered longest here in the hollows and dells, and once or twice in the middle of icy Nonus or even Decius, close to Mithrusmas, Ruby could swear she'd seen flashes of green, gone as soon as she turned her head.

Some things you just couldn't look at straight-on. Especially if you had any Potential at all. Ruby's was respectable, but it hadn't settled yet. She wasn't as high-powered as Gran, or Ellie, but she wasn't low on the gauge, like some branchkin.

Stuck in the middle once more.

"You're quiet. What's up?" Hunter crouched easily, his seal-dark head cocked to catch every sound. As usual, he was a little too close, crowding her personal space.

Kin

Ruby finished tying her trainers and didn't answer.

It was Thorne, as usual, who caught on. "He's coming, isn't he." A lock of wheat-honey hair fell across his forehead; he shook it away with an impatient toss. A flash of white teeth as he grimaced, and Ruby straightened, stretching.

Hunter did too, in a rush. "Who?" He followed as she hopped down from the fallen log, verdant moss blurring its outline. "What?"

"Grimtree clan, one of their brothers. Clanmother's been looking for an alliance for a while now." Thorne wasn't looking *directly*, but he was keeping very careful track of her in his peripheral. Again, just as usual. He'd always been the watchful one.

Like Cami, he watched. Of all the clan, he was probably the one who suspected the most about her—so she kept her distance.

It wasn't easy, when you'd grown up with a pair of boys, to keep them at the right orbit—not too close, not too jealous, not too far. A balancing act, just like the rest of them, speeding up in increments year by year until she looked around and realized the blur was making it harder to keep up.

It didn't help that Thorne was . . . well, difficult.

"Bunch of posers. I hear their Clanmother lets her enemies live." Hunter's laugh was a sharp spear in the gathering dark.

"She's modern. Not like *you*." Thorne got the idea Ruby wasn't going to take the bait, so he tossed out another piece. "Do you remember him, Rube?"

She let it go, touching the closest tree trunk—an old black elm, like the ones near St. Juno's. Leaves rustled, sounding like the tapestry in the living room.

Hunter, of course, couldn't leave it alone. "What was his name? Started with a *K*, right?"

"Conrad. The older twin, by a couple minutes, at least. He's a Tiercey, I think, that's their rootfamily." Thorne's dark eyes gleamed, and he jostled Ruby. It wasn't accidental. She elbowed him back, catching him off balance and slipping away from between them and the tree, their unwitting helper in trying to surround her.

Kinboys liked to fence a girl in. You needed to be quick as a minnow to slide through. Sharp as a shark when they pushed it, too, like they *all* did.

It wasn't their fault girls were so few. Before the Reeve, they'd been born more often than boys. But when the Great War knocked whatever metaphysical cork loose and Potential spilled out to drown the Age of Iron, something happened, and now girls were increasingly rare among the kin.

In the old days, the problem had been mere-humans fearing what they didn't understand and killing what they could. A frightened mere-human was a deadly one, just like the Elders said. Now it was looking like evolution, or Potential itself, was going to do what the Age of Iron couldn't—erase the moon's children.

Behind her, Hunter shoved Thorne, who rabbit-punched him—light taps, one-two, on the arm. They were excited, full of healthy high spirits, just like before every full moon.

"Maybe he'll fight for her." Hunt sounded a little breathless.

"Who cares?" Thorne, bitterly, but Ruby didn't want to deal with his temper tonight. Well, she never did, she hated the constant back and forth, as if she was a bone.

Just one more thing about kin and clan. She lengthened her stride, leaping a bracken-fall, and they hurried to catch up.

The last fingernail-paring of the sun slipped below the horizon, and Ruby took a deep breath. The Park inhaled too, little creaks and crackles in its depths as more cousins arrived. There were a few catcalls from other parts of the Park, the deeper growl of males and six or seven lighter, higher girl-voices. One sounded like Cherry Highgier, who dyed her hair with feyberry red, as if that would make her root instead of just a branch. She went to Hollow Hills instead of Juno.

All the other kingirls did. She'd never had the courage to ask Gran where *she'd* graduated from, or why Ruby wasn't sent to Hills. It wasn't a bad school, but Juno was *the* school for New Haven aristocracy, at least the charm and mere-human ones. If Cami had been born into Family instead of adopted, she would have gone to Martinfield like all the other Family girls. Ruby had once or twice wanted to ask her if she'd ever longed to belong with the kind that raised her.

That wasn't a kind question, though, and she was glad she'd reconsidered, for once. Considering how things had turned out.

Ruby hopped, lightly, testing her trainers. Just right, bouncy in the heels and light in the forefoot. You wanted a broken-in pair, comfortable but with some life left, for this sort of thing. Heels for hunting, boots for tracking, and trainers for fullmoon.

A silver thread ran through the night sky, and like she did every time, she ducked her head and picked up the pace, searching for the right beat.

She settled into a long easy lope, but she didn't follow the thread. Instead, she aimed the long way down the Park. The rest of them could bunch up tonight, but she wanted space and no awkward questions or narrow-eyed judging. Of course, what you wanted and what you got were two different things, even on fullmoon.

The others would ride up the thread like it was a silver rail, pulling the circle tight. You weren't quite helpless in the face of the moon, but sometimes it felt like it. *Rootfamily means freedom,* they said, the strains of the moon's blood in yours stronger, the kin unraveling in branches out on either side.

Freedom? Sure, to a certain degree . . . until responsibility closed in, and your duty to the clan reared its ugly head.

Why are you so Wild? Ellie had asked, once, and Ruby had just shaken her head. Adulthood meant freedom to her friends, but Rube only had a little time before she became a Clanmother-in-training, trying to breed more girls after college so the moon's kin didn't die out, learning diplomacy and how to navigate her clan through alliances, keeping up with Gran's import–export business to keep Woodsdowne a power in the city, and just generally doing everything she disliked until she died.

Ruby sped up. The silver thread widened, and behind her the boys' footsteps fell away. They were branch, too; their mothers had married outclan. Hunter had siblings, all boys, but Thorne was an only. It was probably why he was angry. Without siblings, you didn't have anyone to help take care of your children, and inheritance might pass to a branch with more members after you died. *Cubs need siblings*, the Elders said.

Continuance, every clan's obsession. How many other Wild kingirls felt this desperation? She couldn't just come out and ask *do you ever feel like just a walking incubator for more kin?* None of them had ever been friendly, and Gran sending her to different schools hadn't helped.

Nobody had ever been quite friendly, except Cami and Ellie. Even then, she didn't talk about being kin. There was no point, and the habit of secrecy from the Age of Iron was old and strong. They sort of knew, but they didn't talk about it. Not like Cami and the Family.

Cami considered them normal, and let little things drop. Of course, it probably helped that Nico's father had treated her just like a born-in daughter. It used to make Ruby feel a little funny to visit and see the way the entire Vultusino house sort of revolved around her friend, with Enrico Vultusino clearly thinking she hung the moon and Nico always glowering if he thought someone had messed with her.

Come back to the now, Ruby. You're running.

Hop skip and jump, trainers lightly touching a moss-covered rock, branches whipping by, more sensed than seen. She leapt, ducked, and settled into another lope when she was certain there was a nice, comfortable distance between her and anyone else.

In the distance, the song began. High trillings and long modulated notes, a chorus of communion. Mere-humans would fear the sound, hearing fur and teeth in it, but there was really nothing to be afraid of. It was when the kin were dead silent that you had to worry.

Ruby sank her teeth into her lower lip. A bright scarlet star in her mouth, copper-tasting, the smell maddening and rich. Behind her, Hunter's cry was an orange rose opening against the deepening sky, and Thorne's fierce quiet a song all its own.

When had she started to listen for that silence? Did he guess? Probably not.

Hopefully not.

The end of the Park was coming up. A steep bramble-covered slope studded with stumps and ancient oaks, their leaves rattling as the breeze came up from the bay. Beyond it was the very edge of Woodsdowne, where other suburbs began— Hollow Hills and the Market district, not technically a *suburb* but still not a place to go traipsing while the moon's gift was at its peak. The shift would be on her soon. Already her skin was rippling, a bittersweet pain below the flesh.

He's coming on the train. Furious negation burst out of her, a high chilling note crowding her throat to spillskin fullness, and every kin in hearing distance replied. Harsh, fierce music. Mere-humans used to bolt their doors at night, thinking the moon's children did awful things. They'd more to worry about from each other than any of Ruby's kind, and if you didn't believe that, just look at the tabloids full of mere-humans and charmers doing things to each other kin would never dream of.

All this flashed through her and away in a moment, skating the edge of rage. The red was all through her now, deep like a rosette on the sheets the first morning you wake up with cramp-aches, your body unfurling a scarlet pennon signaling the end of everything good.

Ruby put her head down. Her feet sped up, knowing each dip and rise, the hidden traps in the thornbrakes. A line of fire on her wrist, her cheek, she was going too fast to slow down even as the branches clawed at her.

Another cry, rising from deep inside, and the hill unspooled underneath her. A low stone wall at the top was the boundary, the absolute edge. It wasn't permissible to go past it on fullmoon nights. Woodsdowne was theirs, but outside was the realm of the mere-humans, and on fullmoon, they didn't mix.

Last shot, Rube. You gonna go for it?

Of course Gran said they'd send him back if she didn't like him. But Ruby had a duty. A responsibility.

Why are you so Wild?

They all asked. Why explain?

Breathing hard but smoothly, air like dark red wine, legs full of youth and her jeans shaking off slashing brambles, soles skritching over the top of a stump that still cried out at the loss of its height, a tongueless imperative. A leap, hands catching, bramble tearing . . . and she was atop the low stone wall, as the moon's call sent a secret subtle thrill through all of New Haven, from the sky-scraping piles of rot at the core to the outermost Moving Wall against the Waste, from the highest house on the Hill to the deepest sunken sewer. The bright face and the dark face, and Ruby on the thin edge between them, vibrating, leaning forward, ready to leap—

—and hot iron-strong fingers around her ankle, she fell backward with a blurted cry, all the magic of running draining away.

Back into her life.

• • •

"What do you think you're *doing*?" Thorne, his own skin blurring and the words strangely slurred as the shape of his jaw changed, hissed as Ruby and the brambles both clawed at him. "You go beyond bounds and it'll—"

"FOUND YOU!" Hunter crashed merrily through a wall of greenery, colliding with Thorne. The sound, meaty and solid, would have been hilarious if Ruby hadn't been so stunned. She gathered herself and surged to her feet, juicy needle-fingered vines clutching all over her shirt, weaving in her hair. As if the hillside had come alive, and wanted to eat them all.

"Idiot!" The word spiraled into a thrumming growl as Thorne moved, quicker than quick. The knot of thrashing ended with a flat smacking sound, and Ruby inhaled sharply. They were both on the edge of the shift as well, bulking up and furring out, claws piercing fingertips.

The smells—broken plants, green sap, the baked dryness of stone—held a serrated edge now. Musk, and copper, and spikes of dominance. They both struggled upright, vines hanging overhead like fingers.

"Ow." Hunter shook his head, and there was a flat shine to his dark eyes, visible even in the deepening dusk. "You *bastard*."

Thorne shrugged, and opened his mouth to say something else, probably dismissive.

Unfortunately, Hunter's fist caught him right in the face, and there was a moment of silence after that crunching blow before both of them erupted. Not into vociferous argument, which would have been okay, but into almost-silent motion.

On a fullmoon night.

Great.

Ruby opened her mouth to yell at both of them, but they crashed down the hill in a knot of low deadly noise. Potential sparked: suddenly every vine on the hill wanted to wrap itself in her hair, and the dusk became a spreading bruise.

By the time the others converged on the spot, drawn by that low un-noise of violence and dominance, she had managed to untangle herself and had hauled Thorne back, keeping Hunter down with a stare and a snarl, her lip lifted and teeth tingling. The moon rose higher, a bleached bone dish; for the rest of the evening's run every cousin took turns keeping the two boys apart, and Ruby right in the middle of the pack.

So much for running alone.

FOUR

"UNACCEPTABLE," GRAN SAID SOFTLY. "YOU'VE GIVEN both of them false hope."

Way to slut-shame, Gran. Ruby's lower lip jutted; the Moon was high overhead but the run was done, the shift receding into the place it lived except on special nights. Potential sparked and fizzed between them, describing the arcs of their personal space. Gran's was the glow of an active, powerful charmer.

Ruby's was vivid, sharp-edged, not-yet-settled charm energy pushing against her grandmother's. High emotion disturbed the sea of Potential everyone was swimming in, and it fueled some types of charm, but those were dangerous.

Those were dark, even if not-quite-black charming, and you messed around like that at your peril.

Deep breath, Ruby filling her lungs so she didn't yell in response. When she could talk without screaming, she did.

"I have *not*. They're *cousins*, Gran. We grew up together. You *wanted* me to spend time with—"

"I had thought you would settle with one of them, yes. Obviously that is not going to happen."

So what, if it had, what then? "So I have to get married and start squeezing out cublings right this second? What about getting an education? Am I just going to school so I can be a better barefoot pregnant—"

As usual, Gran took refuge in propriety. "You have a duty to your clan!"

"Why don't you just collar me and chain me in the basement? You could have the boykin take turns and get me knocked up! Then you'd have everything you wanted, right?"

The words bounced around the living room. The tapestry shifted, shifted. Gran had gone white, to match her parchment hair, but the incandescent outrage filling Ruby to the brim didn't permit a step back.

They faced each other, young woman and old, and Gran's shoulders dropped. "I've only ever tried to do what's best." Quietly, as if defensive. But that was ridiculous, wasn't it?

Gran never needed to be *defensive*. She made the decisions, and everyone fell into line.

Ruby's jaw ached with denying the shift. "Oh, I know. For the clan. The clan this, the clan that. It's all about the clan!" A blockage in her throat, a reek of sour salt. Her skin was too sensitive, every edge scraped hard, even invisible air. "Fine! Okay! *Fuck the clan!*"

She didn't mean to scream it, but she did. The buzzing all through her was the shift trying to burst free. Her bones crackled, zinging electricity popping and sparking from her fingertips, her scalp tingling as her hair tried to stand straight up.

Gran actually blinked.

Fury evaporated, leaving only a thin ringing hopelessness. *Uh-oh. Really gone and done it now.*

"I certainly hope you do not mean that." Edalie de Varre drew herself up. "The clan birthed you, has raised you, protected you, given you every advantage."

You raised me. I don't know who birthed me. I don't even know if you're my real grandmother, but we all know I'm root and not branch, I've got to be. Right? The hollow place inside her gave no answer. "So squeezing out babies as soon as I get out of college is a small price to pay for all that, right?" Her hands were fists, to disguise the bulging along her wrists. To shift in front of the Clanmother during an argument, well, you just *didn't.* "Got it, thanks."

"Ruby—"

"I'll be up in my room, preparing to meet my future impregnator. I shouldn't even go to school at all, you know? It'll only give me ideas." She turned on her heel—her trainers were still full of leaf mold and black Woodsdowne dirt—and stamped for the stairs.

"Ruby!" Score one point, at least—she'd managed to make Gran raise her voice.

If it was a victory, it was an empty one. Dirt clumped and scattered from her trainers, all over the hardwood of the stairs on her way up. She'd charmsweep later.

Did I really say that to her? Mithrus.

Her room closed around her with its usual comforting mess, clothes scattered strategically to hide the books underneath, papers stacked to confuse any searcher. Nobody ever noticed the textbooks *or* the fact that she kept all her school notes and reference papers. She should clean the whole thing up and reorganize it now, since she wasn't supposed to be herself anymore. Or even the self she'd made for everyone else.

A bright, careless, exacting child was what Gran had wanted, and Ruby had done her best. Except now they wanted to flip a switch and have a docile breeder. Doing that sort of 180 was enough to make a stomach rebel and a head spin. Even if you were used to flipping around and spinning at a moment's notice for everyone else.

Just thinking about the whole mess made her want to slide the window open and slip out, climb down the plane tree outside her window—an old childhood friend—and then . . . what? She could call one of the boytoys, hit a club, or even just walk aimlessly.

On any other night, maybe. Not fullmoon. Even Thorne wouldn't dare to sneak out and wait around in the Park to see if she was in a mood to run. And if Thorne wasn't coming out, Hunter wouldn't be either.

She flipped the lock on her doorknob, as if Gran couldn't break whatever small pin held the thing in place with a simple flex of her wrist. She was much, much stronger than she looked.

Ruby, although she was kin, was . . . not.

That was the biggest secret of all. Oh sure, physically she was fine, a true daughter of the moon: she could run faster than pretty much anyone, she didn't get sick, and she bounced back after any injury with little trouble.

Gran's strength had a completely different dimension. One Ruby, no matter how hard she tried, couldn't make herself own, too.

She flopped down on her bed. The shaking in her arms and legs just wouldn't go away. Neither would the knot in her stomach.

Here, in this white-walled room with its crimson bedspread and heavy red velvet cushions, she was relatively alone. Only relatively, because every cough, every move, could be heard.

A strong kingirl wouldn't feel this sickness all through her. A good kingirl wouldn't have gone for the boundary wall. A real kingirl would not have shouted *fuck the clan* at her grand-mother.

She was the last hope of the Woodsdowne rootfamily, and all she wanted to do was run like a coward.

No wonder Gran was disappointed.

FIVE

HAVEN CENTRAL STATION HADN'T MOVED SINCE THE
Reeve; the true iron in the tracks and trains kept the worst shifting and Twisting of Potential at bay. You could see pre-Reeve
leftovers everywhere, but they never gave Ruby quite the same
satisfied feeling as the tingle all through her bones as true iron
tamed the often-invisible flux that had drowned the world at
the end of the Great War.

Snowflake-cinders spun lazily down as the train heaved itself to a stop, its blunt nose searching through a cloud of smoke.
The platform conductor was sing-screaming the names of other stops along the line—New Avalon to the north, Pocarello
and points south—and the breakwheel made a grinding noise
as layers of heavy-duty, heavily regimented charm parted. A
delightful, shivery pulsing against all her skin, even under her
clothes, and Ruby was hard put not to shudder. Gran was a
straight, slim iron bar of icy silence beside her, a veil obscuring

her face and her hat perched just-so, only a few hints of parchment hair escaping from under its jaunty tilt.

Ruby was in her dirt-caked trainers, again, a pair of ratty jeans, and a faded, scoop-necked Phib sweater of cerise silk yarn that was nevertheless last year's fashion. No *guy* would get the nuances. Ellie, of course, would know exactly what last year's sweater meant, but she wasn't here.

Thorne stood just behind Gran and to her left, his position as an only child among the branches brought home by his place at the sinister side of the root-mother. Gran didn't hold with much superstition, but she was definitely making a point.

Hunter was right next to Ruby, tucked behind her half a step as diplomacy demanded, the bruising on his face already faded to a yellow-green shadow of itself.

Kin healed fast.

Thorne, scowling under slicked-down gel-darkened hair, couldn't have looked any more mutinous if he'd tried. Still, neither could she, she supposed. Hunter just looked a little sullen.

"BREEEEAK NOOOOOOW!" the conductor yelled, and rivers of charm parted. You couldn't *see* the charm-symbols outright, but the train blurred and wavered under them like pavement under heat-ripples. Billows of steam rose, metal glowing red and the cinders whisking themselves into strange angular cloud shapes before blowing away.

She watched as they began to file off the train, disheveled, with red eyes—recycled air wasn't good for anyone's tender tissues. Still, it was better than maybe getting a lungful of spores or Mithrus alone knew what from the Waste. Part of the high price of interProvince passage, for those who couldn't afford to drive or didn't want to take the risk, was the cost of sealing the iron bullet.

The rest was overhead, and indemnity in case there was a derailment. Sometimes even a lot of iron didn't help out in the Waste. All that Potential slopping around without charmers to shape and tame it, bleeding off the excess, made the risk of Twisting exponentially worse.

Not only that, but there were *things* out there. Dangerous, uncontrolled things, untamed Potential even corkscrewing the flora and fauna. That was why they called it the Waste.

A shape looming through the steam. Her spine knew before the rest of her, a zing like biting on tinfoil all the way down her back. Ruby inhaled, sharply, and Thorne tensed beside Gran. Having them both here was vintage Gran—she thought it would give them a lesson. Friendly rivalry was okay, but anything even a fraction of a step above that was frowned upon.

Because it could hurt the clan.

He was taller than her, ink-black hair cropped aggressively short. A strong jaw, the familiar high cheekbones, and a kin's supple movements. There was an oddness about him, rasping against her instincts, but then, he was from another clan and would naturally smell a little . . . strange.

Did he feel the trap closing around him, too?

A flash of mellow gold. Even among the moon's children his gaze would be called spectacular. Sun-eyes, too warm and deep to be yellow. Bad-luck eyes, glowing like the Moon's sister-enemy.

Uh-oh. She tried to remember if anyone had said anything about that before. He had a brother; did they have the same eyes?

He carried a single large dun-colored duffel, easy grace and broad shoulders handling it like it weighed nothing. A wilted blue button-down, sleeves rolled back to show tanned forearms, a pair of jeans just as thrashed as hers, and very nice boots. Ellie would know the brand off the top of her head, but Ruby just took in the quality of the stitching and nodded internally.

There was a clan cuff on his left wrist. Wide age-darkened leather with silver snaps, the Grimtree crest stamped deeply and creased. Something about the cuff seemed a little weird, but he bowed properly to Gran, just enough insouciance mixed with the respect to denote strength.

He was *definitely* dominant. Just how dom remained to be seen.

"Clanmother de Varre." A nice deep voice, and Ruby's entire body flamed, a scalding icebath. "Grimtree sends greetings, and respect."

The veil stirred at its edges, either from a slight movement or a stray bit of breeze. When Gran spoke, it was just above a formal murmur. "Woodsdowne returns the regard. You have changed much, young Conrad."

"Almost fifteen years will do that. Except to you. They say Woodsdowne is as beautiful as the Moon."

Ruby's jaw almost dropped. Was he *flirting*? With *Gran*? The boy straightened, and *boy* was a relative term. He was nineteen, but damn if he didn't seem, well . . . pretty effortlessly self-possessed.

"Some branches are always blessed. Thorne, please take our visitor's bag. Ruby."

"Gran." She kept her feet right where they were, although she was supposed to step forward to greet him as well.

That golden gaze turned to her. Cheeks hot, her messy hair every which way, why had she deliberately not even combed? Or washed her face? There were probably crumbs on her chin from dinner or something.

His pupils dilated a little. Ruby watched, fascinated, as her tiny image in those black holes vanished behind the shutters of his eyelids. He even rocked back a little on his heels, and the whole rest of the train station went away. For that moment, there was just the two of them, and a broad white smile rose on Conrad Tiercey's face, a crescent of perfect teeth.

His bag dropped with a thump, almost as if he couldn't hold onto it any longer. "It's true," he said, just to her. "More beautiful than anything."

It should have been cheesy. It should have been a warning.

A tightness she hadn't even been aware of loosened in Ruby's chest. The smile on her face felt dopey, but she didn't care. "Hello." *Oh, my God, is that really all you can say? Good one, Ruby.*

He swallowed, visibly. "Hi. Ruby, right? Conrad."

She held her hand out. He stepped forward and took it, gently, strength underneath. His skin was warm, rougher than hers. A slight movement, as if he wanted to kiss her knuckles, but that was old-fashioned. So they just stood there until Gran coughed.

Ruby found her throat was dry. "Moon's greeting," she managed, traditional words of welcome. "How was your trip?"

"Boring." The smile returned, a private joke. "I had to make my own fun."

She grinned back, and it felt completely natural. "I'll bet."

"You are most welcome here." Gran took a single step forward, and Conrad dropped her hand. "Our guest is no doubt exhausted. Thorne—yes, thank you. Hunter, please take word to your mother that he's arrived safely; the Elder Circle will want to know."

"Yes ma'am." Hunter bumped into Ruby as he went past—not hard, but not accidentally either. There was a line between his eyebrows, and his mouth was pulled tight. "See you later, Rube."

"Sure." Later, she would think back and notice how he'd

looked worried. The breeze shifted, and she caught a good whiff of healthy male kin, a fascinating new scent without the underlying musk and black earth of Woodsdowne.

There was a harsh angry undertone that should have raised her hackles, but all Ruby felt was a raw unsteady relief.

Maybe this wouldn't be so bad after all.

SIX

"WHAT'S HE LIKE?" ELLIE'S BREATHLESSNESS WASN'T about the news, of course. Rube got the idea she'd almost forgotten about today's Big Event, and it had taken a little while for Ellie to run to the phone. Which meant some uncomfortable small talk with Avery Fletcher while they waited for Ell to show up and release them both from torture.

It wasn't that she didn't *like* Fletcher, it was just that . . . well, he wasn't Ell. Or Cami.

He wasn't *safe*. No mere-human really was, but her friends were . . . safer. At least, she'd always thought so. The thought that she might not be safe for *them* was uncomfortable, and it kept circling nowadays, just like everything else.

"He's tall." Ruby twisted the cord around her fingers. Her closet was small and stifling, but carrying the phone in there was such a habit she barely noticed anymore. It was dark, and color-coded outfits—she kept the closet door closed to hide its neatness—brushed her head. "Nice smile."

"Okay. But what's he *like*?"

She could imagine Ell hopping with impatience, the phone to her ear and her pale hair a wind-rippled drift over her shoulder. It was almost white now, and some of the girls in summer school thought she bleached it. Ruby could have told them she didn't, that the color had been *drained* somehow . . . but why bother? Let them gossip. "He went straight to bed. Still sleeping. I don't know yet, but he seems . . . nice."

The line crackled with a short silence. "I don't think I've ever heard you say that about a guy before."

That's because most of them aren't. "Well, Gran plans to marry me off to him, I might as well look for something to like."

"Yeah, about that." Ell's tone dropped, became worried and confidential. "Are you sure you're okay?"

Danger, kiddo. If she drew Ruby into talking, Ell would figure out a few things, not the least of which that she was terrified. Really, Ell didn't need that kind of thing when she was settling into her nice new life with the Fletchers. Mithrus knew she deserved all the help she was getting now, just for suffering through the hell that had been her stepmother.

So Ruby put on the cheerful, careless voice again, familiar as an old coat. "Whoops, gotta go. I can't make our date today, got to show him around town. Tell Cami, will you?"

"Ruby—" Ell didn't give up easily.

"Maybe tomorrow. Ciao!" She hung up and shut her eyes. Comforting darkness, fabric softener and her own scent, familiar as that lying, cheerful voice. Conrad was in the spare room next door—had he heard her? Had Gran? God, this place was so *small*.

Gonna have to get used to it. Collaring made the world even smaller. They were made in two parts, collar and key, and if you were good your keyholder would let you take the thing off for short periods. She'd seen collared kin before, the thin, liquid-silvery gleams cinched tight around their vulnerable baseform throats. Thin and nervous, with a haunted, faraway look, denied the shift and a kin's sensory acuity.

Would Gran actually, really do that to her?

If I disappointed her enough, maybe.

She used to be so *sure*. Petted and told she was the rootfamily's hope, Gran's heir and bright star, given primacy among all the cousins as a matter of course . . . and there was this looming thing in the distance that she hadn't really thought about as a kid. Hope depended on her marrying, spawning, and taking Gran's place.

Maybe she'd just had too good a time and now had to pay for it. Was that what *adulthood* really meant?

Nothing was certain anymore. First Cami had started acting odd and vanished into that nest of pale, dripping foulness under

New Haven, then Ell had fled her stepmother and ended up with that fey thing, and neither of them were the same even though they'd been dragged back. There were shadows in dark corners, and Ruby was always saying the wrong thing.

Try not to be a selfish bitch, Ell had flung at her, last school year. *I realize it's your default, but just try.*

The worst thing, the thing that hurt the most? Ellie was right. If Ruby wasn't so selfish, she wouldn't be feeling this way. She'd be grateful for the clan, and it would be small potatoes to give back to it. *Clan is kin and kin is clan*, as the old saying went, and you were nothing without that net.

She should have been grateful. She should have been just *aching* to get her marriage settled, get through college, get knocked up and assure her place in the whole goddamn thing. You weren't a real Clanmother until you had at least one kid. You could be just a regular old Tante, but the clan would be adrift after you died until the Moon gifted one of the branches with a sign of Her favor.

"It's going to be fine," she whispered to her clothes. She wanted for nothing. Gran's allowance for her was really comfortable, to say the least, and Ruby never even had to whine to get what she liked.

A cage with a nice lining was still a cage. Still, she owed Gran, didn't she? She owed *everyone*. Because the clan had birthed her, raised her, protected her—the list went on and on.

Clan. Like *adulthood*, it was one of those words that seemed cool when you were a kid, but then it shifted and ran around howling.

Movement elsewhere in the house. She strained her ears, listening. Footsteps too heavy to be Gran's, not as precise.

He was awake.

The padding footfalls paused outside her door. Ruby gapped her mouth, breathing silently. Would he think she was weird? Her door was solidly closed, but could he sense her in here? Nobody else hid in closets just to talk on the phone, did they?

He kept going. Down the hall, familiar squeaks and creaks odd now that someone new was making them. If she was a good kingirl she'd probably have been downstairs already, making breakfast. She'd probably already know how he liked his eggs, too. She'd be making him feel comfortable and doing all the boring hospitality stuff.

Did she want to impress him? Or did she want Gran to send him back to his clan and maybe pick someone else? Maybe even someone old enough to be her father.

She'd worked up the courage to ask Gran directly about her father only once, but the old woman simply pinched her mouth shut and shook her head, slightly. The way her steely eyes lightened was enough to warn Ruby off the subject for a good long while. Oncle Stephen had been buzzed at a barbecue later and told her that her father was *really* outclan, which was probably true. Stephen wouldn't say more, and none of the other kin could be induced to talk about it. Except for Gran once saying that he was outclan, and that Thorne or Hunter weren't close enough to give the bloodline problems.

If Hunter knew, he'd probably tell her; Thorne wouldn't be able to stop tormenting her about having a secret. It was more likely that even the branchkin just didn't talk about it.

Ruby eased out of the closet. Her room, with its new and unfamiliar neatness, closed around her. She hadn't even made her bed yet. As a delaying tactic, that kind of sucked, because it would only take three minutes.

Then she would have to go downstairs and make small talk.

She waited, listening, heard a formless murmur of conversation. Footsteps again. He was wearing shoes, sounded like boots. The front door swung open, then closed with a quiet, definitive thud.

Wait, what?

The kitchen was neat as a pin, the only marker of Conrad's presence a cereal bowl in the sink. He must have scarfed it pretty quickly, but probably with good manners, seeing as how Gran was at the kitchen table, frowning at a layout of playing cards. Kings, queens, jacks, and charmers, red and black and white, familiar glares on the slick much-handled surfaces.

Her braid was perfectly in place, but there were shadows under her eyes. Her dragon-patterned housedress was almost long enough to conceal her embroidered slippers, and her back was ramrod-stiff as always.

"Good morning!" Ruby chirped. "Is he up yet?" As if she didn't know.

"He said he did not wish to intrude upon us this morning, and left to visit with kin." Gran's mouth was a straight line while she finished a thought, the lines bracketing it deeply graven today. "He remarked that you might be . . . shy."

For a second Ruby just stared, the words refusing to make sense. Then a laugh slid out sideways, hiccupping in the middle as she tried to pull it back. Gran's barely noticeable frown deepened.

Still, she couldn't help herself. "Well, at least he's polite."

"You are not *shy*." The old woman looked down at her cards. Sometimes charmers could see things in the patterns, though Ellie often sniffed and called such divination unscientific.

At least Gran was talking. Maybe she'd forgiven Ruby for the other day. "Not with people I know." Nettled, Ruby swung the fridge open. "Or people I *want* to know. What do the cards say?"

"Not much." Gran's strong, slim fingers moved quickly, brushing the laminated rectangles together into a neat stack. "Sometimes they are silent."

She snagged the orange juice. His fingers had touched the milk carton. At least he didn't hang around and try to be awkward or funny with her in the morning. He was giving her a little space.

Maybe this whole thing was just as weird for him as it was for her. What if she didn't measure up? Sending someone back was one thing.

Being rejected was something else entirely.

Guess that makes me shallow. For once, she didn't drink straight from the carton. She also wondered if he'd looked for the glasses, if he'd opened this cabinet or that one. If Gran had told him, *To the left of the sink, young man.*

She took a deep breath. "Do you like him? Will he do?"

Gran eyed her for a long moment, as if Ruby had started shifting right in the middle of the kitchen. "Do?"

She kept an eye on pouring into her glass, pretending to be absorbed in the simple task. "Yeah, are his clan connections good enough? Will he negotiate passages and tariffs well? Do you think he'll be an asset?"

"Such questions."

"Well, that's the whole point of this exercise, right?" She concentrated on pouring. "To further the clan. So, do you think he'll be an asset? He's got a twin brother, right?" *So there'll be even more of a bond there to ally us with the Grimtree, which will make intercity trade easier. Might shave a few points off tariffs.*

"This is quite a change." Did Gran actually sound *uncertain*? Nah, couldn't be. "Might I ask what brought it about?"

"If you don't like it, I can go back to being a brat." She shrugged, and popped the fridge open again. "Seriously, though, you're right. I owe the clan everything. I could have died as an orphan for all I know. So if what it takes is me promising to marry this guy, okay."

"You are no orphan."

Did you adopt me? You never talk about it, and nobody else will either. "Hey, when is he coming back? I should drive him around. Or should I go wherever he went? He's probably visiting the Ardelles first, you think? Didn't they have a Grimtree marry in?"

"I am surprised you remember."

Ruby took a deep breath and tried again. "I remember *lots* of stuff. Anyway, yeah, there was a Grimtree girl who married in. Sonja. Car accident, when I was eight. Everyone cried, and you led the run through the Park."

There had been gossip afterward, too. That Efraim Ardelle had threatened to collar Sonja, and that it hadn't been a car accident, but an escape attempt. She'd been heading for the province border, if the whispers were true.

Which was really interesting. Oncle Efraim was a lean, dry-eyed, hatchet-mouthed kin, and some whispered that he believed his nephew Peter should resurrect the old, old ways and share his mate with the head of his branch—at least, as long as they were childless.

Poor Sonja, everyone said. And, *It's a good thing Tante Rosa isn't here to see this.* Tante Rosa, Efraim's mate, had passed on after a long, mysterious illness, and sometimes Ruby caught whispers about *that*, too. Rosa had been held to have certain relationships with the fey, and some of Efraim's hardness and lack of kinfeeling was blamed on that.

The end result of all that clan history brought up a new, uncomfortable line of thought. A handsome young Grimtree wasn't the worst that could happen. What if there was a way-older guy in another clan seeking alliance, one bitter-mouthed and stone-hard like Oncle Efraim? There might be overriding reasons to promise her in marriage to someone else.

There was always Hunter, and Thorne. It hadn't been until middle school that they started the rivalry dance. If all else failed, maybe she could take one of them? Since she had to put up with someone. Maybe Hunter. He was pretty easy to redirect, not like Thorne.

Thorne had *never* been easy. And if she was honest, she liked that he wasn't, even if she would probably pick Hunter just to make things . . . safer. Smoother. Less intense.

Gran sighed. Of all her sighs, this one was the most patient. "Sonja was . . . fragile."

I know how you feel about weaklings. "Everyone says she was nice. But seriously, should I go over to the Ardelles'? Or should I wait for him to come back? What's the etiquette? I know I should know, but I don't." *At least I know not to ask him about dead kin. Awkward.*

"Either is acceptable. Ruby, I know you feel our clan way's might be . . . old-fashioned. I don't wish for you to think I'm blind to the fact that the world has changed, and the kin must change with it."

What did that mean? Orange juice, tart and cold, slid down her throat in long swallows. Was it Gran's perennial, *It could be worse, don't complain*? Or maybe it was, *There's a way out, I won't force you.*

Who knew? Gran almost *never* changed her mind, and she had said out loud it was time for Ruby to start thinking about the future. Her future. The clan's future.

And other things. *I should collar you, to save you from yourself.* It echoed in the space between them, where before there had been only comfort and warmth. Sharptooth words, snapping and silent growling.

Ruby rinsed the glass and gave her best, sunniest smile. "We're all modern now. I'm going to go see if I can catch him at the Ardelles'. You going into the office today?"

"Yes. Ruby, I wanted to ask you—"

Mithrus Christ. I'm doing what you want, all right? "Yes, I'll do my chores, yes, I'll be nice to him, and no, I'm not going out with Cami and Ellie. That about cover it?"

Kin

Gran's shoulders relaxed a trifle, though she looked like she wanted to say more. "I suppose it does. Be careful, child."

"I'll be with kin. Nothing's going to happen to me." She blew Gran a kiss and danced out of the room.

Being responsible and cheerful was exhausting, and she wasn't anywhere near through yet.

SEVEN

SHE DIDN'T HAVE TO GO FAR TO FIND HIM. HE HADN'T gone to the Ardelles' at all.

Cami and Ellie often professed amazement at her ability to simply *find* things, whether it was the "in" accessories each school year or the honeywine coolers nobody else could score. It made her writhe a little inside each time, first with embarrassment and now because when it had really, really mattered, she hadn't been able to find either of them.

Ellie had been the one to find Cami with that dowsing-charm of hers, and later, it was Avery Fletcher who had found Ellie with that fey creature. Both times Ruby had honestly tried, running all over town, sometimes with the cousins and other times alone, searching for the tingle that would lead her to her friends, the worry under her breastbone a deep tar-black pool. She could find a pair of shoes, a missing kitten, the best accessories every school year, but when it counted, she'd come up empty.

Kin

In other words, she'd failed them both. Just like she was probably going to fail the clan.

It was a relief to follow her nose and pull up at the edge of the Park, and a double relief to see Conrad's short black hair. He'd hopped up on the near wall, a thigh-high tumbledown stone affair facing onto Tooth Street. He sat, broad shoulders hunched, and something inside Ruby tightened a little.

She knew what that felt like.

He didn't turn around when she cut the engine, or when she got out. The Semprena gleamed, its finish charmwash glossy, its windows blind eyes. It was a lovely little car, with sinuous black curves and comfortable bucket seats in front. The shelf serving as a backseat wasn't huge, but that meant more speed, and she liked that just fine. Ruby could still close her eyes and see Gran's face as she handed over the keys the day after she passed her initial driver certification. *This is . . . an heirloom. Treat it well.*

She had. It wasn't just four wheels and an engine, it was *freedom*, of a certain type. Maybe Gran had understood that.

She settled on the wall next to Conrad, not too close but not too far, her back to the Park. That way he wouldn't have to look at her, either.

Neither of them said anything. The silence wasn't dangerous, but it was taut. A faint breeze whispered through the trees, redolent of the knife-edge between late summer and the beginning of harvest season. A dry brown scent, not juicy green like summer's height.

Finally, he shifted a little. "I should be visiting kin, shouldn't I."

"They'll still be there tomorrow." She kicked her feet out, lazily, staring at her shoes. They were cute little Sendij strappy sandals, really darling, and the crimson polish on her toenails wasn't chipped at all. The fashionably frayed jeans and her crimson tank top might send the wrong message, but she looked all right.

Fat lot of good it did, since he kept staring at the Park with those sun-colored eyes. "I might not be."

"Going home so soon?" Didn't he like her? He'd called her beautiful. Her stomach knotted itself up.

"Maybe. Maybe I'll strike out into the Waste. Better than sitting around, waiting for the axe to fall. Letting *them* run my life."

Did he mean his clan, or just elders in general? Either way, she couldn't argue with the sentiment.

Or was he saying she wasn't enough to stick around for? Just making conversation? "Would you really?"

"Shit. I'm sorry." Now he looked at her, sideways but still a long, lingering glance. "That's really insulting, isn't it."

"Yeah, but I understand." Her legs dangled, shorter than his. "I don't want them running my life either. But what can you do? It's the clan this and the clan that, and everything just . . ."

"Closes in on you. Like a collar." A thoughtful nod. "Until you have to do something. Anything, to get away."

Thanks for mentioning a collar. There was no way for him to know about Gran's threat. Maybe someone had thought he was troublesome enough to be threatened with it, too. "Yeah." She stared at the Semprena's curves. Both Ell and Cami thought she drove too fast, took too many chances. How could she ever explain to them that behind the wheel was the only place she felt like she might actually have a shot at escaping?

"You're not what I expected," he continued. "I thought, another spoiled kingirl. Instead, you're, well, different."

Thanks. "I'm plenty spoiled. Just ask Gran."

"Everyone's afraid of her."

"Well, yeah. She doesn't control trade through the Waste by being cuddly."

"Guess not." He was still as a stone. "Do you like her?"

She caught a breath of well-oiled leather from the clan cuff, his healthy musk, the angry smoky smell underneath. Something about that low burning set her on edge, but she couldn't pinpoint why. Maybe it was just that he was from another clan, or maybe it was because he was taller than her, and heavier.

She wondered if Cami or Ellie ever felt small around Nico, or Avery. "She's my Gran." *She's all I've got.*

"But do you like her?" .

"Most of the time." No point in lying. *Sometimes I don't, but I still love her.* "Don't you like your Clanmother? She's your grandmother, right?"

"Her? I hate the bitch." Softly, but it sent chills down Ruby's spine. There was a snarling under the words, not quite dominance but not quite rage either. "Always ordering people around."

None of the Woodsdowne cousins would *ever* talk this way. At least he was being honest, not pussyfooting around how he felt. Still, Ruby had to close her mouth with a snap before she could find something to say. "That's sort of her job, though, right?"

"Not when her orders are stupid. And my parents just go along with her, and . . ." He shifted slightly, as if he wanted to lean toward her. Went back to stillness. "Look, you don't have to pretend. You know, be nice to me. I'll make it clear it's not your fault if I leave."

I don't know what'll happen if you leave. "Like anyone will believe that." Her palms were wet, and her heart pounded. "I'm sort of a problem."

He turned his head, and his eyes were darker, and hot. The look was a physical weight along the side of her face, but she kept staring at the Semprena. Sunlight rippled in its paint, hazed off the pavement in the distance down Tooth Street, tingled against her skin. As long as she wasn't shifted, it was a good friend.

The smoke underlying Conrad's scent faded, whisked away on the breeze. "Me too. Hey."

She waited, but he said nothing. Maybe he'd used up a significant proportion of his courage, and it was up to her to take the next step.

So she did. "What?"

"You know how to drive that thing?"

She tried not to roll her eyes, and only halfway succeeded. "No, I just sit in it and look pretty. Of course I do."

A flash of something dark marred the handsomeness for a moment, but she didn't see it. "Smart girl. Where do you want to take me?"

PART II:

DANGEROUS PATHS

EIGHT

IT WAS THE FIRST TIME ANYONE REACHED OVER, grabbed her arm, and shouted, "*Faster!*" His fingers sank in almost to the bone, the pain a silver wire like the moon's call, and each time she jammed the accelerator to the floor.

They did one of her favorite loops—up to the top of Haven Hill, a zigzag through the empty Market district—Monday meant no Market—with each of the traffic lights turning amber in a vain attempt to slow her down. Slewing sideways, through the shabby gentility of Falada Place and finally onto Woodsdowne Loop, flashing through liquid treeshade and bright dappled sun. The oaks—old as the Reeve, in some places—flashed by in a semaphore of stodgy trunks, heavy branches, the leaves envious of her fun but tethered to the larger mass. The right onto Tooth Street was so familiar she could have drifted into it in her sleep.

A long slide of burned rubber, the car trembling just at the edge of her control, before both left-hand tires came to rest gently against the curb right where they had left an hour and a half ago, the stereo blaring Tommy Triton's old *Blackhall Jack* album drenching them both like rain, ignored. When she cut the engine, the sudden silence was stunning, the car still rocking slightly.

Ruby blew out a long, satisfied breath. "Welcome to New Haven."

He was pale, but two spots of livid color stood out on his cheeks. It suited him, even if he was a little too thin. A train ride would do that to you, though—even the rich had trouble digesting out in the Waste.

He blinked a couple times, and his jaw worked. Looked like he was having trouble finding words. His irises burned gold, and he blinked rapidly. "You always drive like that?"

No. You just get the special treatment. "Pretty much."

"Dangerous. If you can't handle it."

Thanks for your concern. "No accidents yet."

"Good thing." He was slowly turning a regular color again. "This city's kind of small."

Well, maybe, if you're from New Avalon. She said nothing, measuring the steering wheel between her crimson fingertips. Her polish was chipped on her right thumb and left ring finger, and it bothered her. Nothing ever stayed fresh; it all got rundown and ugly.

"You like Tommy Triton?" Did he sound tentative?

"He's okay." All of a sudden she wanted to be home in her room, on her bed, with the music blaring and nothing on her mind other than a couple gossip mags and some nail polish. Maybe it was time to try another color.

"Kind of middle school. You ever listen to Kraxhead?" Did he sound hopeful?

"Nope." *I thought only feyhempers and Dust addicts liked them.*

"You should. They're good." As if he was doing her a favor.

Maybe he thought he was. Ruby pushed the irritation away. "I'll look them up." The green blur of the Park was a heavy weight against the windows, and the sunshine through the windshield made sweat prickle along her hairline. "I should take you to the Ardelles'. Or back home. Gran'll know we're not visiting kin."

"Does it matter? We're together."

For a moment she couldn't believe her ears. A flush started on her throat and worked up to her cheeks.

"I mean . . ." Now he sounded awkward. "We're both, you know, problems. That's sort of why they sent me. I mean, sure, I'm rootfamily . . . but I don't do what they want."

"Me either." She swallowed dryly, rolled her window down. The good crushed-green of cut grass flooded the car—someone had mowed recently. "I'm going to try, though."

"Why?"

"Isn't that what growing up means?" *If I manage to mate and breed at least one kid I'll be Clanmother when Gran's gone.* And if she didn't, the clan would be rootless after Ruby's lifetime, until the Moon made a junior branch into root, bringing dominance and some physical mark of her favor to the surface.

He shrugged. He was too big for the passenger seat; the Semprena felt a little too small with him sitting there, shedding healthy heat-haze. "According to them, I guess. Can we . . . you want to go for a walk? I like talking to you."

A different warmth all through her. He was a stranger, and it sounded like the deck had been pretty stacked on the "don't-like-this-girl" side. If he liked her, really liked her . . .

Well, he might be the first person who ever had. Even Cami had taken a little time to warm up to her, and that was after Ruby had taken on all comers in primary school, picking a fight with anyone who made fun of the shy, scarred girl's stutter. And Ellie . . . well. Of course Cami got along with Ell, Cami could get along with anyone if she wanted to. It'd become Ruby's job to protect them both when Ell's family moved in from overWaste, and she'd done her best.

Ruby was useful, and she was in the same social circles, and she could find things. They had *reasons* for liking her. The cousins, well, they had to act like they could stand her, at least, because rootfamily were due that much. Others—like the other girls at school—couldn't afford to piss her off, because she had that temper reputation.

What would it be like to have someone want to hang around without a reason? She'd always wondered.

"Sure." She jangled her keys, popped the lock, and glanced over at him. "You don't have to, you know. I'm hard to get along with."

"I think I'll manage," he told her, and later she would realize it was a warning.

At the time, though, she just grinned and swung the door open, stepping out into summer's last breath.

"Kind of small." He hopped up on a fallen tree, its moss dry and brown since the fall rains hadn't started. "Don't you ever want to run more?"

Ruby shrugged. She hung from a convenient low branch, enjoying the stretch. Tensed her stomach, drew her legs up a little, checking her toenail polish again. There was a certain charm to pedicured toes against the roughness of bark and leafmold. Civilization and wildness all in one. "During Mooncall, sometimes I just want to hit the wall at the north end and keep going."

Parallel to the log he perched on, the boundary of the Park was a clipped green verge along the street. He kept trying to go further in, but Ruby kept to the outside, where she could see the fronts of branchfamily heads' houses. There was Oncle Sanvord's, blue with white trim, and the lime-green Harvrell house—probably crammed to the gills with boycousins this week, since Tante Freya was sick and couldn't care for her brood right now. They would all be out helping with Gislain Harvrell's construction work, keeping them out of trouble until school started.

Conrad nodded. "Maybe you should. You ever think about it? Just running through the streets and showing them how to be afraid?"

She dropped, lightly, and brushed her hands clean. "That's taboo." The breeze was redolent with mown grass and the faint cinnamon undertone of leaves exhaling before they started to turn.

"All sorts of things are taboo. I just wonder." He hunched his shoulders a little, staring into Woodsdowne's depths.

"You get Twisted if you do taboo stuff." It wasn't *quite* precise—the Moon taking her blessings back wasn't the same as Potential corkscrewing you into a wreck of your former self.

Close enough, though. Enough to make you shudder.

Conrad shrugged. Dappled sunlight all over him, he moved restlessly and touched the clan cuff, as if it irritated him. "We don't Twist with anything else."

"Well, no, but there's the stories." *And really, the taboo stuff is just common sense. Don't eat human flesh, don't breed with your siblings, don't hurt each other.* "About the things that happen when the Moon—"

"You believe in that? It's just a hunk of rock."

"Well, yeah, *scientifically* it is, but there's a meaning—"

"You ever think that maybe the taboos are just to keep us from asking questions? Finding things out? Being what we really are? I mean, *them*. Charmers and idiots, soft and pink, without even the sense to stay away from bad meat . . ." Now he was looking at her, expectant, obviously wanting her to agree. Or maybe just thinking she *could* agree.

Whoa. "Um." Ruby searched for something tactful to say. Of course Cami or Ellie could come up with something that didn't sound like an insult, but that wasn't one of Rube's greatest strengths. Graceful conversation was pretty much always a waste of time.

Still, she had to try. "I never thought about it that way," she managed, finally. "They're not all bad. I have friends who aren't kin." *Good friends.*

Best friends. It wasn't their fault everything was shaking them up and making them grow apart.

He shrugged. "Yeah, well, they'll turn on you. You can't trust anyone."

Wow. "Not even your own? I mean, you have a brother, right? And your parents, and—"

"They're happy to send me off. My brother . . ." Conrad hopped down. "Never mind. I'm being rude again. Let's walk."

"Sure." Relieved, she fell into step beside him, ambling

along the grass just at the border. "You're not rude." It sounded a little strange. "I mean, I can understand."

"You'd be the first, then." He cut her a sideways glance, half his mouth tilted up in a wry smile, and she found herself smiling too.

Maybe she was getting better at tact.

NINE

CRICK-CRACK. PEBBLES RATTLING AGAINST GLASS.
"Rube!" A whisper-yell. "Come on, open up!"

Rolling over, her room unfamiliar in that trembling instant between sleep and waking. They'd rambled all around the Park twice, and returned home smelling of sap and fresh air. Gran hadn't said a word about the kin visits not happening, and Ruby's amazement was only matched by Conrad's slow smile.

See how easy it can be, that smile said. It was enough to make her half believe he might be a solution.

Or at least, the best option to happen along yet.

"Rube, come on!" The whisper-yell, again, and a rattling.

What the hell? She pushed the covers back and winced a little as her arm twinged. The bruise was already fading, but Conrad's grip was strong. That sort of strength was scary and comforting all at once, like Thorne's fierceness.

Speaking of Thorne . . . A thin frown tilted her lips; she slid out of bed and padded to the window. Two quick tugs on the sash and it was up, night pouring in with an edge of chill. The plane tree just outside, with its convenient branch she'd used more than once to clamber out and explore the night, rustled under a heavier weight. Of course, he was taller, and wider in the shoulders.

"What are you doing?" she whispered, fiercely. "Gran will *kill* you."

"Only if she catches me." Thorne's expression was a thundercloud, his hair a wild mess. In the dark, he was almost brunet, and his dark eyes were merely gleams. "Where were you today?"

"Showing my guest around. What the hell are you *doing*?" It was one thing for her to sneak out and meet the cousins on the corner or in the Park's depths. It was an *entirely* different thing for him to be at her *window*, for God's sake. His familiar scent, dark with an edge of musk, flooded her nose. The usual relief loosened her shoulders—she couldn't have put it into words, how seeing him sometimes made the world steadier. It slowed down the whirling.

Even if she had the words, she wouldn't have told him. There was no point in making him think . . . well, *things*. Thinking things only caused trouble.

Right?

He leaned forward, almost breathing in her face. "Wanted to talk to you. Have you seen Hunter?"

"Not since the train station. Why?" She braced her palms on the sill and leaned out, whispering.

"He's . . . something's wrong with him."

"Other than the usual?"

He glared, leaves stuck in his hair like a fey's autumn crown. "There's nothing wrong with him *usually* except he's not dom enough for you. We all know it. Look, did he call or anything?"

"Nobody's dom enough for me, Thorne." She chewed at her lower lip, wished she hadn't, because his gaze fastened on her mouth. "What's wrong?"

"Hard to explain. Can I come in?"

"Are you insane?" She cocked her head. Was there a soft sliding step, somewhere in the house?

Thorne didn't make any indication of hearing it. Instead, he plunged ahead. "I might be. Look, he says there's something weird about this Grimtree. He doesn't smell right, and I agree. Been thinking about it. Shouldn't he have a sub around to keep him company and brush his boots? Maybe even his brother?"

That *was* traditional, but Ruby hadn't thought about it. Trust Thorne to find something to worry about. "There's not enough room in the house for *another* male. Maybe Gran told them so. Maybe Grimtree wouldn't send two root boys to look at one root girl. It might give the wrong impression. But seriously . . ." Ruby sighed. "This is it? You and Hunter don't like him because I'm supposed to pick someone in-clan?"

"Want you safe. And happy." Thorne shrugged, the branches rustled alarmingly. His T-shirt was torn as if he'd been in a fight, but then again, he didn't care about clothes. It probably drove Tante Carina to distraction, having to wash and mend for him. "I don't think Hunt *or* this Grimtree can do either."

"Which just leaves you, right? And if you get caught here, I'll get into trouble, Conrad will have to go home, and you can claim we've—"

"What kind of guy would do that?" He was forgetting to keep his voice down. "Is that really what you think of me?"

I wouldn't put it past you to act first and think later. God knows that's your default setting. "I think you're not supposed to be here. Mithrus *Christ*, Thorne, you're such a jerk." How did he manage to irritate her so thoroughly every five minutes? It had to be a talent.

"Glad to be. You'd eat a nice guy alive, Rube." He shifted again, leaning back, and the branch creaked. "So you haven't seen him."

"Nope. No call, no visit, zilch, zip." Now she was starting to get worried. It was ridiculous, though. Hunter was just on the edge between dominant and submissive, right in the middle of the pack. It wasn't like him to go haring off and do something stupid. He was usually the voice of reason when she dragged both of them out to have some fun. "What exactly are you afraid he's doing?"

"Getting himself into trouble. Same as you." He eased back. "Be careful, okay? That Grimtree, something's *off* about him."

"He's perfectly nice," she retorted as hotly as she could in a whisper. "He likes my driving!"

"Then he's crazy." He winked and was gone, dropping out of the tree to land soft as a whisper.

The irritation mounted another few notches. She longed to climb down, follow him, and smack him on the head, just to do it. The old Ruby would have.

The Ruby Gran wanted her to be now, though, wouldn't. She quietly closed the window and tiptoed back to bed, listening intently.

Nothing. The cottage was still and silent, not even the static unsound of someone awake. With Thorne vanished, the place was an oyster shell, closed tight around her as a pearl. She could be the only living thing left in New Haven, and wouldn't know it until morning. Unless she crept down the hall to check if Gran was still breathing, like she'd done as a little kid.

What a great thought.

Her arm hurt a little. She glanced in the mirror, seeing the dark print of Conrad's fingers. Thorne hadn't noticed, thank Mithrus.

Not that she was worried, but something warned her it was probably best if she kept the two of them apart. Maybe she should add Hunter to that list. Juggle all three of them like a street busker throwing sylph-ether globes. Just don't drop any-thing, because that would be a mother of an explosion.

Under her tangled mop of hair, she was smiling. It was a se-cretive expression, and she watched as her eyes danced and her teeth peeped out just a little, glowing in the half-light. It was late, the waning moon no longer pulling on that silver thread, and when she climbed back into bed she no longer felt so alone.

TEN

Two days later, she took a deep, surreptitious breath and tried again.

"They're my friends." *Even though they're not kin.* She tucked her feet underneath her on the couch. Sunshine hadn't begun to come through the living-room windows yet, so the bronze lamps were lit, and the tapestry, for once, was silent. "You'll like them. Cami doesn't talk much—she used to stutter—but she's really smart. Ellie, well, she's super-smart too. All practical and shit, too."

"Vulgar." But Conrad said it with a smile, lounging in the overstuffed royal-blue easy chair Gran never used. "There's time later. I want to get to know you."

Which was nice, and made a traitorous little bubble of warmth rise under her sternum, but still. She itched to be *out*, doing something. "This is a good way to get to know me. We can't hang out at home forever."

"Why not?" He stretched his long legs out, as if the living room wasn't too small for him.

At least if she got married she'd have a house of her own. The space might be nice, except Ruby was neutral on the subject of cleaning. A certain amount was necessary and nice, but *doing* it was a pain and best done quickly and thoroughly. She'd be responsible for meals too, and while she *could* market and cook, well, it wasn't exactly her cup of tea. There was so much else you could be doing.

Like wheeling over to the Vultusino mansion and lounging by the pool on a glorious sunny late-summer almost-afternoon. "There's obligations. You know, social."

His expression darkened. His booted feet played with the round leather footstool, pushing it a little further away as he settled more firmly into the chair. "We both hate those."

I only hate some of them. She reached for diplomacy, yet again. For two days she'd been making small talk with him, and though he generally had something interesting to say, it was beginning to get a little . . . well, boring. "But they're *obligations*. Anyway, my friends are different."

He shrugged. "Can't we go for a drive?"

No. "You just want to drive my car."

"She's a nice car." He grinned, fondly, as if the Semprena was his and he was proud.

Nobody drives her but me. "If you don't want to go, that's fine.

Kin

Gran should be back in an hour." The Valhalla Bridge Club used to play marathons, but lately things had been serene enough that they met, played a few tricks or some mah-jongg, drank tea, and had long meandering discussions about tariffs and trade agreements, gossip, and whose child was going to make a good match or had done something naughty.

They weren't all Woodsdowne. Gran's usual partner was a dowager from the Stregare Family—one of Nico Vultusino's extended kin, a mover and shaker among the Seven. There was Mother Gothalle, an old, slightly dotty Sigiled charmer who lived near the core and had an agreement or three with the fey to bring certain things through the Waste. And iron-spined old Queenie Falada, whose family had been in New Haven since before the Reeve. Ruby didn't know what Mrs. Falada imported *or* exported, and she was pretty sure she didn't want to.

Sooner or later, she'd probably have to. Maybe after college. Which was creeping up on its stilt-legs, closer and closer all the time.

Conrad, having settled the footstool just right, stretched out his long legs again. "You've gotten tired of me." His mouth turned down, and he scratched at the clan cuff like it itched him.

"No, I just want to see them before school starts." It was, she decided, good practice in being patient. Gran was endlessly patient, when she needed to be.

"Schoolgirl."

He probably didn't mean it as nastily as it sounded, but she bounced up anyway. "Have fun staring at the walls. You're going to miss seeing me in a bikini."

"Don't go." He didn't move, just sat-sprawled with his golden eyes half-lidded. Somehow she got the idea he didn't quite want her to *stay*.

It took her thirty seconds to clear the house, and she twisted the volume knob all the way up. Tommy Triton was wailing about shaking down the walls, and even if it was juvenile pop, she sang along while the Semprena's engine purred.

Up on the Hill the Vultusino mansion was a massive weight of gray stone, but the pool was a clear blue eye, surrounded by lovingly tended gardens and a cheerful little poolhouse with two changing rooms. Warm brick walkways and pale scrubbed concrete were always safe to walk on, and the water was heavily charmed to the right temperature.

Cami settled, dripping, into a teak lawn chair. Even just risen from the glimmering water she looked polished, her hair a river of ink, her lips glossy red, and her pale skin gemmed with clear droplets. "Some s-sort of charmclan thing. Ell was bummed."

The sunshine was just right—not too hot, because of the steady breeze. The red bikini was an old friend, a veteran of plenty of afternoons just like this. Ruby wriggled a little with pure delight. "Well, at least Avery will be there to keep her company."

"You don't like him." Her blue eyes dancing, the Vultusino girl looked amused. She usually did, when it was just her and Ruby. Anyone else added to the mix upped the worry factor.

Maybe she found Ruby super-soothing.

Yeah, that'll be the day. "I like him fine as long as he makes her happy."

"Speaking of which. This Conrad." Cami's expression had turned slightly anxious, eyebrows drawn together and her pretty mouth tilting down at one corner.

Ruby shut her eyes. Sunshine all over her, a delicious buzzing, and each little drop from the pool against her skin was a tiny mirror-dot of sensation. "We have two days before school starts again."

"You're avoiding."

So let me avoid. That wouldn't fly. Cami would just worry. Her anxiety was a silent static, and it wore against the nerves.

Maybe only Ruby would hear it. She shifted slightly, the red glow through her closed eyelids a thin screen between her and the world. "The whole thing is boring. I'm supposed to pick someone to settle down with long-term, preferably while attending Ebermerle so I don't get tempted by any charmcollege boy hotties, then get married and squeeze out enough babies that the future of the rootfamily is assured."

"Aren't you kind of . . . young for that?" Carefully, as if

Cami wasn't sure how far she could press. Her usual deck chair was shaded, and she would be sitting with her knees drawn up, hugging them. Just as she usually did.

"I won't breed until after college. But really, not all of us live forever." It might have been unjustified, but she couldn't help herself.

Cami was quiet for a long moment. "It's n-not forever."

The scars might be gone, but a ghost of the stutter remained. If it had been someone teasing her, or something physical, Ruby could have beaten it up or made it go away.

You couldn't fight some things, or solve them. They just sat there, hurting the people you loved. Forcing you to juggle faster and faster to keep everything from crashing down. "Family *is* forever. So is clan." *Both of them add up to a trap*, she added inside her head. *At least for me.*

Another long moment of silence. Was Cami watching her with that pitying look? That was the trouble with the Vultusino girl. She felt everything all the way down, and it made the world outside the walls dangerous for her. She needed protection.

That used to be Ruby's job, at least at school. She only had a year left before she was fired, so to speak.

The thing was, with Cami scar-free and not stuttering—much—anymore, and Ellie out from under her evil stepmother and doing fine, Ruby might be terminated from the only job she outright *liked* a lot sooner. Thrown out like a sudden Twist, suddenly no longer part of the tiny group she'd tried so hard to earn a place in. Her own little corner of the world outside the clan.

"Family." Cami sighed, very softly. Her chair was under a white sun umbrella, and it creaked a little as the wind touched it. "It means a lot of things."

To you, maybe. Ellie wasn't getting the crap beaten out of her almost daily, and Cami was no longer so painfully, incredibly vulnerable. She was damn happy about both things, she really was.

There was just another feeling mixed in with that happiness, a hot, unsteady one. "It does, you're right." Ruby essayed a smile. It felt odd against her face, like the mask it was. "You got some booze?"

"Honeywine coolers, as usual." The chair squeaked as Cami rose. "I'll talk Marta out of them."

"Good deal." She heard a slight exhale, and her eyelids flew open. "Look what the cat dragged in."

"De Varre." Nico Vultusino, lean and tall, his moss-green eyes squinting slightly against the flood of afternoon sunshine, appeared like a revenant at the edge of the white-painted pool-house. Even in a white V-neck and jeans, he'd never look like a cabana boy. That edge of danger and old red copper to his scent raised all her hackles, and he liked it that way. "Nice to see you."

That's a lie, Family boy, but thank you. For Cami's sake, she contented herself with a noncommittal noise. "Mh."

"Nico." Cami, small and slim and fearless, padded barefoot toward him. "Did something happen?"

"Will you stop worrying? It's handled." His teeth flashed in a very white grin, and he leaned forward. Just a little, as if he were a plant and Cami the sun. That slight, subtle movement told you everything you needed to know about them. "Everyone's all friends again, at least until the next time that damn Canisari makes a fool of himself."

Ruby's throat threatened to block itself. "Great. You could make yourself useful and bring us some booze. And something for yourself," she added hastily, congratulating herself for the politeness. "We could sit around and talk about nothing."

"Sounds nice." He reached out, and as soon as Cami got in range, his hand polished her bare wet shoulder. "You okay?"

For a moment Ruby thought he was asking *her*, and a laugh threatened to spray all over the pool. Water lapped; she swallowed the sound and realized he meant Cami.

"F-fine. What exactly happened?"

He shrugged, nice and easy, but his gaze came up over Cami's shoulder. The warning was clear.

Don't talk in front of strangers. "Tell you later," he said. "I'll get you some coolers, then, if de Varre over there won't snitch to her grandmother."

"She would *never*—" Cami began, hotly, but he laughed and tugged gently at a lock of her long black hair before vanishing down the path leading to the house.

"He likes pulling your chain," Ruby observed. "So, the Canisari? They're pretty reckless. At least the younger ones." For a little while she'd had a crush on one of them, but that embarrassment was something she'd take to the grave.

Family and kin didn't mix. Except Cami, and her. They were exceptions all over, weren't they.

"Oh, yeah. So's Nico. He's getting better, though." Cami turned, standing in the shade of the poolhouse, and her eyes were a blue glimmer. "Ruby, can I ask you something?"

"Ask away." A long, luxurious stretch. Maybe she'd avoided the rocks. If Nico came out, Cami wouldn't question her about Gran or Conrad or anything else. They could do the old familiar dance, Nico trying to get a reaction, Ruby giving him one, Cami keeping the peace.

Just like always.

"Do you really like this Conrad guy, or is it just what you have to do?"

Nope. Not past the rocks yet. "Talking about it is *boring*, darling. Leave it alone."

"Okay." Cami came back, picking her steps with care on hot concrete, and Ruby suppressed a sigh.

The pressure mounted until she had to speak again. "It's just a betrothal. It's not the worst that could happen," she added. "Really. Trust me on that."

Cami paused, looking down at her. In the sunshine, she glowed, an alabaster statue. Her swimsuit—white, one-piece, she'd stopped wearing cover-ups all the time—was rapidly drying. "You d-deserve more than that."

It's sweet of you to think so. Another smile. "Thanks, Cam. It's getting hot. Race you to the pool." She was off the chair and halfway to the water before Cami laughed and bolted after her.

ELEVEN

"I'M *HOOOOOME*!" SHE CALLED INTO THE COTTAGE'S cool, dark interior. "Did you miss me?"

No answer, but the house didn't smell empty. Gran was inside.

Great. Had she been supposed to sit here and babysit Conrad? Had he decided to go back to New Avalon? *That* would be just grand, wouldn't it.

The lights were on in the kitchen, and Gran was at the table, bolt-upright. Her hands were folded, and Conrad was there too, leaning against the counter near the sink. His expression was indecipherable, sun-eyes gleaming under the electric glow. They hadn't had dinner yet.

It's not my day to cook. What's going on? "Gran?"

"Ruby. Sit down." The lines on Gran's face were graven a little deeper today. Instead of one of her housedresses, she was in her office wear, a black silk shell and tailored pants, a summer-weight wool blazer draped crookedly over the back of her chair.

It wasn't like Gran to hang something up that way. Especially her work clothes.

"What's going on? What happened?" She glanced at Conrad, but he was no help. He just stood there, staring at her. Was that a smirk? It couldn't be.

"Sit down."

"I want to know what's happening." She folded her arms, her stomach turning into pure acid. "You said I could go to Cami's today."

Did Gran's mouth pull itself even tighter? "And if I call her, no doubt she will confirm you were there."

Hot injustice, then, but she supposed Gran had a reason. She'd caught Ruby sneaking out a few times, including the last and most memorable when Rube had been trying to get out on a fullmoon night, desperate to hunt down missing Ellie and thinking that maybe with the *shift* burning in her she could find what nobody else could.

Or maybe it was something else. Gran hadn't mentioned collaring again.

Was it that? But she'd been so *good* lately. "You can even ask Nico. But I suppose you think he'd lie for me, for Cami's sake. I'd go to those lengths to cover my tracks, right?" She shrugged. "Okay, fine. What is this?"

"Ruby . . ." Gran took a deep breath. "When did you last see Hunter?"

For a moment the words made no sense. *Why is everyone asking that?* "At the train station, when we picked up Conrad." She looked at him, but the Grimtree was no help at all. He just watched. The world gave a little jiggle underneath her, but she didn't have any attention to spare to figure it out. "Why?"

"Sit down."

The floor was acting funny, and there was a buzzing in her ears. It was her body again, knowing before the rest of her.

She pulled out her usual chair and lowered herself into it, slowly. "Gran, what's happened?"

"We found Hunter." Gran's hands tightened against each other.

Then why are you asking me . . . She couldn't even finish the thought. Sweat prickled all over her. "Found him?"

"In Woodsdowne Park, in the heart of the green. Ruby, he . . . he has gone to greet the Moon."

What? The roaring in her ears made it difficult to think. "That's impossible," she said, with perfect logic. "He's a *cousin.*" *He's young, and we don't get sick often. When we do, we fight hard. Like Tante Rosa.*

Gran was very pale. She'd only looked this way once or twice before. "He was attacked."

What? Her mouth was numb all through, as if she was

buzzed on something stronger than honeywine. "Attacked? You mean . . ."

"Yes. He . . . Hunter is dead, Ruby. He . . . he fought, but something—someone . . . I am sorry."

What? Numb, she stared at Gran's familiar face, turned alien now. She kept talking, but all Ruby could hear was the roaring. Maybe it was the honeywine coolers, though kin didn't get drunk really, just pleasantly slow for a little bit. The simple sugars burned off with the poison of alcohol, a little lassitude and then you were done.

She could still smell the chlorine from the pool in her hair. Her bikini was still in the car, too. She had to go get it out. Plus there were chores, right? Chores to do. There had to be. This was all a mistake, and if she just did her chores . . .

"Do you understand?" Gran, quietly and firmly. "Please, Ruby. I am so sorry."

There was a hand on her shoulder. It was Conrad, and he squeezed. He didn't know his own strength, because it hurt, badly. A crunching, grinding pain.

She didn't wince. She just stared at Gran's familiar-strange face across the table.

"In the Park." A good schoolgirl, repeating her lesson. "Hunter . . . in the Park. He's . . . dead. Who . . . Gran, who would hurt *him*?"

"We do not know." Gran's irises were the color of steel, now. "But when we do, there will be justice."

TWELVE

NEW HAVEN SWELTERED UNDER A LID OF GRAY, HEAVY cloud. Wet flannel, pressing down on everything below, steaming its way into every pore. The trees drooped, even though their green turned deep and vibrant like a jungle; the ones that had begun to turn stood halfway painted, splashes of color on their branch-fingers as they shivered feverishly.

In the old days, the kin would have been deep in the woods, and a platform would have been built in the treetops. The body would be arranged carefully among the sap and leaves and sawdust, and birds would clean the bones. After they were naked, white bone would be stained with ochre and wrapped securely, then returned to the earth.

The Age of Iron left great scars in the old forests, and the Reeve had made them Waste. You couldn't have bodies hanging in the treetops in Woodsdowne Park—although, right after the Reeve, sometimes they did.

For those reasons, and others.

Her charmhose stuck to her legs. White-sleeved long dress-
es on the women, Gran's patterned with subtle dragons in ecru
thread, Ruby's linen plain of any ornamentation. You couldn't
wear an underwire or jewelry, no metal allowed. Even silver,
that holy Moon-glow ore.

No metal, and no words. The kin buried in silence. This
graveyard was within New Haven, but no inspectors or city
groundskeepers came within its peaked iron fence. Gran
had once remarked that negotiating the passel of restrictions
and leases with City Hall had been delicate and patience-
consuming, but worth it.

Those leases had been negotiated just a little after the Reeve,
in the vast deep darkness of the Deprescence; Ruby never quite
figured out if Gran meant she'd been there to witness it herself.

Absolute silence as Woodsdowne men related to Hunter
and past their tenth fullmoon run carried the wrapped body,
thin sapling-sticks sewn into the wrappings to provide support
for the cloth and the antistain charms.

Her lips moved a little. It was probably blasphemous, but all
she could think of were the chapel songs at St. Juno's. *Mithrus
Christ, watch over us all; we are the lambs and you the shepherd. . . .*

Gran never said anything about Juno being run by the
Mithraic Order, though the kin remembered darker times
when anything remotely churchlike was dangerous. Even now
cathedral-kin was a dirty, serious insult.

It meant *betrayal*. It meant you'd given one of your own

Kin

to the mere-humans who once hunted kin for Church and sadistic pleasure alike. A tremor went through Ruby; she braced herself against the nightmare.

It was no use. There was no waking up from this.

Even though they had wrapped . . . him . . . carefully, it was still pretty obvious that things were, well . . . The shape was wrong, bulging oddly near the head and the legs too thin.

Things were missing.

What had *happened*? Gran just said, "He was attacked." Conrad said nothing. Nobody else would tell her, and Thorne . . . well, he didn't talk, or visit.

At all.

Something moved next to her. She couldn't stop thinking about chapel at Juno, the girls massed together, Cami with her sweet throaty alto and Ellie, when she bothered to sing, quietly but clearly hitting every note. They made it sound easy.

When Hunter was eight he had announced she was pretty okay, for a girl. The smoky char-smell of barbeque and the tang of lemonade on her tongue, she'd let him kiss her cheek and the adults had laughed. Of all the cousins, he was the sweetest. The calmest, too—he'd only gotten into a domfight a handful of times, and all of those with Thorne.

It was Thorne next to her, dry-eyed and tense. The movement was his hand on her shoulder, warm and familiar. Her knees almost gave.

Hunter's mother, dun-haired Tante Alissa who had married

out to a branch from the Cherweil clan down in Pocario to the south, swayed. Her husband Barth propped her up. Hunter's brothers, all older, were either carrying the . . . carrying him, or standing on their mother's other side. Gran, apart and alone as Clanmother, held the silence as the slow steps of the bearers drummed on sweating earth, crushing green grass.

They lowered him slowly with charmed straps of seven-braided linen, and the soft thump of him resting against the bottom jolted all through Ruby. She bent forward, suddenly breathless, Thorne's arm around her shoulders. He held her on her feet as the charmed shovels lifted soft steaming earth.

Gran reached the graveside and looked down. Her old, strong hands lifted, their nails unpolished and a little long, gleaming slightly. Potential buzzed between her palms, a shower of colorless sparks fountaining into the hole in the earth. You could see layers in the sides of the hole, stripes of different-colored dirt like pages of a book.

Ellie would know what each stripe was called.

The gravecharm settled in fine gossamer layers. Hunter's mother sobbed, but silently. Until he was sealed, there was no speaking, no sound if you could help it.

He had to be free to go on, and speaking would call him back. Words crowded her throat. *This is a mistake. Hunter, it's a mistake, one of your pranks, stop playing around!*

He loved water. Always the first in the pool, and sleek-graceful as a seal.

Stop it, Hunter. Stop it.

Gran stepped back and nodded. The first shovelful was tossed in by Hunter's eldest brother, lean, dark-eyed Robert. His wife wasn't here—she wasn't kin. If they had any children it would be a miracle, since kin and mere-human were often sterile pairings. Just one more unraveling of the bloodline, but at least there was a chance she'd give birth to kin.

Maybe even a girl.

Crunch of shovel-edge against the pile, the soft sound of it pattering like rain into the hole. Ruby straightened slowly, but Thorne didn't let go of her. His arm around her, tight and tense, but not digging in. Her hand quested a little, blindly reaching for the grave, but Thorne reached across, grabbed her wrist with his free hand. Was she trying to pull away?

He held on as if she was. The world whirled, hot and muggy, her breath coming in short little sips. A green carousel, going too fast.

Thorne's arm tightened again, just on the edge of pain. He leaned into her, and for once she didn't step away. If she pressed her side against his, the whirling slowed a little. It didn't stop; nothing would stop it. It just got easier to handle.

The bearers worked, mechanically. Her cheeks were wet.

Hey Rube, want to go to the Park? Hunter's dark, sleek head, and the way he ducked and smiled, shyly, each time she saw him. Wrestling with Thorne in the Vultusino's pool, cocking his arm to skip a rock across the pond they'd hung out by the summer of her seventh-grade year. The time he gave her bluecharm candy for Fish Day and laughed when she found out it was sour. She'd once fallen asleep against his shoulder as they sat in an arcade on Southking, watching the crowd pass through the window. He hadn't moved the whole time, barely even breathed.

The mound of earth shrank, shovelful by shovelful. Each load of dirt crackled with Potential. Bindcharms, sealcharms, some already worked into the dirt by Gran, others bound into the hafts of the shovels and escaping in controlled bursts. When a shovel's charms were emptied it was laid aside and a fresh one handed to the bearer; each family of each branch had at least one they added charms to at every fullmoon.

If the bones must be laid in earth without being cleansed, at least they would be laid securely.

When the final load had been tamped down, the still-charmed shovels were laid aside as well. They'd be drained as dusk fell, and next fullmoon the charms would begin accreting again. Back during the Reeve the shovels were consecrated daily instead of monthly, the Moon taking pity on her children and providing them a little grace as the Age of Iron shuddered to a halt.

A glass bowl of silence, laid over the hilltop. The last funeral she remembered was old Maxim Corris, not the head of his branch but still the one everyone went to with problems because the head, Gregor Corris, was, well, a little harsh.

The Corrises had always been strange; they were full of

fierce silence, the Moon's daggered hand instead of Her giving palm. But Oncle Maxim's interment had not felt like this.

Gran half-turned. Her steely gaze met Ruby's. She tilted her head, very slightly.

Dry throat. Shaking, as if she had a fever. Ruby stared back, willing her knees to stay steady. Gran would be seeing Thorne's arm around her, their fingers knotted together.

Would she smell the grief spreading from him like a bruise, red-violet pain digging into her ears and nose? Over his living scent, musk and male and fresh-cut grass, would she catch that fringed screen?

Gran didn't understand.

Well, really, nobody understood Thorne, mostly because they didn't care to. If he'd had at least one sibling, it might have been different. Maybe. Or maybe he would be just as spiky and difficult. They called him *Thorne* instead of his given name, even his parents—Hunter had started it, sure, just to be funny about his real name, but some things had a habit of sticking. His mother, willowy blue-eyed Tante Carina, had a hard labor with him and was rumored to now be barren, but his father made no move to take another mate. Nobody mentioned doing so to him either, not since he almost broke Oncle Radin's jaw for even suggesting it during a clan meeting.

That was probably where Thorne got his temper. Under that temper, though, he cared, probably—like Cami—too much. Nobody saw that under the anger he wore.

Gran's gaze moved on. She nodded to Hunter's mother.

Alissa tilted her shorn head back, her eyes closed, and the sound that rose from her thrilled into the ultrasonic. A glass cry, a moon-cry, even under the daylight it twitched the silver thread inside Ruby's bones.

The rest of them flung their heads back and howled.

It was a different hymn than one of the music-teacher Sisters picking at the organ, and different than the thudding of Tommy Triton's backup drums too. High, hard, and silvery-haunting, it rose and fell in cascades as the breath did, each voice unique but their similarity overpowering.

Ruby's mouth was open, but no sound came out. Thorne's hands were strangely gentle. His throat swelled, the shine on his cheeks wasn't sweat. Hot salt smell, and finally, finally, the shame in her own throat eased aside long enough for her own cry to join the rest. It went on and on, echoing against the uncaring daytime sky.

Underneath, the same dreadful knowledge beating against her cathedral-arch ribs, under her heart. Over and over, the same two words.

My fault. My fault. My fault.

Because maybe he'd been waiting in the Park for her, like he often did. All her sneaking out at night had a price, too.

THIRTEEN

ALWAYS, AFTER THE SINGING, CAME THE GATHERING. The Corris branch's head house was a nice two-story brownstone, facing the Park, its large backyard now full of kin. The firepit was going, though it was still hot, and there was the smoky smell of meat being charred. Red paper lanterns hung in the trees and from the grape pergola, the Mackenroe twins had tubs of cool water to dip washcloths and rags in. A crackle of a coolcharm, and the icy rag could be patted against the neck or the forehead, providing a little relief.

Under the pergola, the heat was just as intense as in the middle of the yard. At least the thought of dappled grape-leaf shade helped.

Ruby hunched on a collapsible stool, bent over, her arms crossed tight over her midriff. Thorne laid the cold cloth against the back of her neck. "An axe," he said, finally, under the crowd-sound around the fire pit. When dusk fell the Remembering would begin, stories told of Hunter's life, because *now* he was safely with the Moon. If any piece of him had lingered, it had ridden their cries to the sky, past the sun's veil to the round, pale Mother of All. "I heard Clanmother talking to my father about it."

Why your father? "An . . . an axe?" The nausea just wouldn't quit. "Oh, Mithrus."

"Like Gaston Wolfhunter." Maybe he just had to say it. "That's why she was talking to Dad. He did his dissertation on those feytales."

"Feytales aren't real." Except Ruby had seen one, living and breathing, underneath New Haven last winter. That particular feytale had almost killed Cami. And the other thing, the fey-spider that had lured Ellie in and almost eaten her? Another feytale, maybe. Legends and myths peering through the bars of the Age of Iron, come back to terrible life.

"Doesn't mean someone crazy isn't wanting to carve some kinflesh like old Gaston." Thorne's lips skinned back from his teeth, a humorless grin. *"In the dark of the Moon, when the wind is high, and the wolf cry fills the night—"*

She shivered. "Will you stop? That's just *gruesome*."

"Yeah, well." He took the cloth away, refolded it. A cool-charm crackled, and he pushed her hair aside, laid damp coldness against her nape again. It felt wonderful. "You want something to drink? You look a little pale."

"I'm fine." If she said it enough, maybe she'd believe it. "You go ahead if you need to, though."

Kin

"Rather stay with you." His other hand brushed at her hair, as if there was something in it. "You guys were . . . close."

"So were you." She licked her dry lips. "Thorne, do you think . . ." *How can I ask him? Where do I start?*

"All the time." Softly. "Can't get away from it."

She almost winced. That was part of his problem: he just never stopped chewing at himself. If you got him occupied with something, he'd dig until he hit gold or blood. There was no stopping him once he got an idea. "What do you think he was doing in the Park?"

The bubble of their silence grew. She half-twisted to look up at him, but he was staring in the direction of the firepit. Cicada buzz, high in the trees, rasped under the sounds of somber conversation and the crackle of the fire. Her stool wasn't too steady, and the brick floor under the pergola was veined with moss. It would serve her right if she slipped, got dumped on her ass here.

Conrad appeared at the back door. He moved aside, letting someone else pass, and surveyed the backyard. He looked straight at her, and his mouth turned down a little.

Her heart squeezed in on itself, then thumped up into her throat. It was doing a lot of moving around these days.

"Probably meeting someone," Thorne said, finally.

Probably. Was he waiting for me? Hoping? She dropped her head. Thorne's even, careful stroking of her hair continued.

"Here comes the Grimtree." He didn't sound happy about it. Ruby hunched her shoulders.

"Ruby." A wash of healthy boykin smell, and that tang of smoke underneath it. Maybe it was just the firepit. "I was looking for you."

"Well, now you've found her." Thorne's fingers tightened against the cool cloth. "Lucky you."

"I didn't catch your name." Conrad sounded interested and pleasant, but that edge to his scent intensified.

"I didn't give it." Thorne's smell grew stronger too, dominance rising, unwilling to back down.

Conrad's smile didn't change. "Do you have a problem, Woodsdowne?"

"Not yet." Thorne patted the coolcloth, and Ruby put her hand up to hold it without thinking. "I'll get you something to drink, Rube." He brushed past Conrad, and Ruby looked up just in time to see the Grimtree boy shoulder him, a little roughly.

God, would they ever stop the dom games? All the boykin were like that. Maybe it was hormonal. Testosterone poisoning.

Thorne, however, just kept walking. Conrad stuffed his hands in his pockets, the clan cuff digging into his tanned flesh. He looked down at her, and heat suffused her cheeks.

"I'm sorry," she managed, peeling the cloth off her nape. "He and Hunter . . . they were best friends."

"Looks like he's pretty friendly with you too."

She couldn't tell what his tone was. It wasn't quite angry,

was it? "He's clan." Why did she feel like she was lying? "Are you . . ." *Are you all right?* It sounded ridiculous, so she didn't finish. Why wouldn't he be okay? It must be awkward for him, but that was about it.

"I'm packing."

It refused to make sense. "What?"

A shrug. His eyes had darkened a bit, and he wouldn't quite look at her. "Well, you know. I'm not exactly welcome here."

"What?" *I sound like a cuckoo bird. Or a complete idiot.* Either was pretty likely. The dress clung to her; she couldn't change until she went home. "I mean, what makes you think that?"

"Well, you've got all these obligations. I'm just in the way." Was that a nasty twist to his mouth? Or was he just grimacing with embarrassment?

"Are you serious?" She twisted the rag in her hands. A thin thread of water slid out, touched her knee. It didn't help. She was going to sweat right through the linen, and probably drip all over everything just like a kelpie fresh from its pond.

"Well, it just looks . . ." A sudden stop, and when he went on his tone had turned into something softer. She couldn't quite figure out how. "You've got a lot to deal with here, and the last thing you need is more pressure. You know?"

Great. Now Gran was going to think she'd made him feel unwelcome. She would get that disappointed look, and . . .

For once, Ruby's imagination failed her. Her skirt was going to get soaked. She loosened up on the rag, took a deep breath. The fire pit smoke stung her eyes. "I'd like you to stay." She couldn't say it very loudly, but at least she'd put it out there. "Please."

A rustle went through the assembled kin. The sun was sinking, and soon it would be time to eat and tell stories. Except she didn't think she could swallow a single bite.

His shadow changed shape as he crouched. "Hey. Oh, Christ. You're crying."

"S-sorry." She bit her lip, hard, but the blurring wavering in her eyes refused to stop. "I d-don't usually." Was this what Cami felt like, when she stuttered? She knew what she wanted to say, but it got all racked up between brain and mouth.

"Shhh." He pulled her forward. Her knees hit the bricks with a grating jolt, but she didn't care, because he put his arms around her and there was a dark space to hide in. For some reason, that was what did it, breaking the shell between her and a roaring sea.

Ruby buried her face in the Grimtree's shoulder and sobbed, as quietly as she could. He stroked her hair, clumsily, pulling at the curls a little. The rag fell on the mossy bricks, and she didn't see Thorne's return, or the way he stood at the edge of the pergola watching.

She didn't see Conrad's expression while he stared at Thorne, either, or the narrowing of those sun-eyes. His hand caught in her hair, she gasped, and he immediately started murmuring soothing things—*sorry, go ahead, cry it out.*

The Gathering went on until midnight, with stories and songs and feasting. Stories of Hunter's pranks—the Mithrusmas he locked Thorne in a closet, the time he threw a popcharm in the fire during another clan gathering and scared everyone to death, his love of fizzy limon drink and his taste for coral candy. So many stories, falling into the black hole that was his absence.

Conrad loaded up a plate and pressed her into eating. She kept looking around, seeing familiar faces, but not the one she wanted.

Thorne had left.

FOURTEEN

THE FIRST WEEK OF SCHOOL WAS MUGGY AND GRAY as well. It was the only week last-years couldn't drive in, and Gran was at the office all day. Conrad offered to drive her in the Semprena, but it was bad enough that Gran had decreed he was going to *share* her car.

He is our guest, Ruby.

Inside St. Juno's, charm-cooled air moved sluggishly through the high-ceilinged halls. Lockers slammed, hushed giggles ran around like tiny mice, chalk scratched on the boards, and the chapel was full of an incense hum.

It was like she'd never left.

Except things had changed. Ellie's Potential was settled, so she'd moved up into Advanced Charm instead of Basic. Wonder of wonders, Cami's had too, between one day and the next. Sometimes it did that, and they were in Advanced Charm together.

Which meant Ruby only saw them during chapel, French, and High Charm Calc. The rest of the time, she was on her own, and it was not only deadly boring, but it was also . . .

Well, it was lonely.

There were prepgirls fretting over their socialite status, and bobs—the new girls, still finding their way around. The ghoulgirls with their black hair dye and heavy eye makeup, but no lipstick, because that was *too* far outside the rules, playing at being black charmers. They sometimes gave Rube a shiver— she'd *seen* a black charmer, in summer, during the hearing that had banished Ell's nasty-ass stepmother. It wasn't something to play at, even if a radio show or two had reverse-heroic black charmer characters.

Ruby slumped in the wooden seat, trying hard to concentrate on Sister Margaret Ever Loving's drone. At least she wasn't sharing a desk with anyone. Her reputation was good for something. Or maybe it was just Gran's reputation, or Woodsdowne's.

"The forties were a decade of migration and war." Sister Margaret, rail-thin inside her billowing black robes, leaned on the podium. Her right cheek was seamed by a long thick scar, and she sometimes wound her rosary up in her long bony fingers as if it were a throat that needed crushing. "The Deprescence was over, but its effects were long felt. Who can tell me what those effects were?"

Migration, nationalism, economic patterns shifting. Ruby held still, and the Sister called on blonde Binksy Malone, who blinked and simpered her way through the answer. It was pretty impossible that she'd done some studying over the summer, heavy partier that she was. She kept glancing at the textbook the whole time, and Sister Margaret let her suffer.

God, just move on. Ask another question. She scribbled on her notepaper, slowly drawing loops inside loops. It was no use.

An axe, Thorne had said. She'd managed to piece together a little more at the Gathering, and afterward, when visitors kept coming by the cottage. They didn't come right out and say it in front of her, but if Gran could hear every sneeze in the house, it was pretty stupid to think Ruby couldn't hear the low voices in the kitchen or living room.

Legs cut off. Marks in the flesh. Charring around the edges.

They even whispered it, the name of the most awful thing in the world. *Gaston Wolfhunter.*

Sometimes during history class she considered standing up and telling the Sister running it that there was another textbook, written in the bodies and voices of the kin. They remembered things. How it was to be hunted, or to burn at the stake during the Age of Iron. How it felt to huddle in your bed at night hearing the scrape of an axe haft on your window. Sure, when you looked it was just the tree's branches.

It was a kid's story, all right. A feytale, like the Impossible

Riddle or *Crusoe, Man-Eater*. Except there was history under the sheet of legend. There *had* been a Gaston. Several of them, in fact. Way back before the Reeve, in the very beginning of the Age of Iron, the Mithrus Catolicus had trained mere-humans to recognize kin and other things, like fey.

Which would have been okay, except the recognizing was only so they could kill. *A frightened mere-human is a dangerous one.*

"Miss de Varre?" said Sister Margaret's dry, dusty voice.

Ruby came back to herself with a jolt. "What?"

Whisper-giggles.

"In what year was the Compact of Provinces signed into law?"

Oh, that's easy. "Thirty-nine, Sister."

"What was the purpose of that compact?"

"To facilitate trade as well as solve the problems inherent in governing multiple enclaves surrounded by the Waste. Communication and the normalizing of relations were critical if enclaves were going to survive."

The Sister nodded, and turned her entire body to look at the clock over the door, its heavy glass and wire covering buffered to prevent charm reaching through. It was a wonder she didn't creak. Maybe she took oil baths, like grinmarches were supposed to.

"I am relieved to find you paying attention, despite all appearances to the contrary." She turned back, slow and ponderous despite her thinness. "Required reading tonight is textbook chapters three through five; your first essay of the year is due at the end of the week. It must include at least two of the following . . ."

Ruby sighed, scribbling down the list of requirements. Of course they'd load you up the first few weeks. Revenge for summer freedom, maybe.

At least she wouldn't have to think. She could just do her homework without bothering Cami and Ellie over Babchat. It used to be the high point of her day, her fingers racing over the keyboard, the blue glow on her face, talking through cables to her best friends. On the Juno intranet, Cami didn't stutter and Ruby didn't have to slow down, plus you could access some of the library without having to stick your beechgum somewhere for safekeeping. It was a pretty perfect method of communication. There was talk about extending it through buried lines, maybe even getting different cities and towns to Babchat to each other, but nobody had figured out how to do *that* yet. Potential and electricity had weird effects on each other.

The circles she'd been doodling nested together, and in their center two curves looked away from each other. Between them, a slender handle daggered for the bottom of the page.

Labrys. An axe. Her stomach filled with acid, and she shut her eyes and tried to breathe, until the charmbell tinkled and they were free to go to their next little purgatory.

• • •

"Hey." Ellie slid into the seat between her and Cami. "How are you?"

"Peachy." Ruby stared at the textbook. "I sense a quiz coming on."

"It's only the first week." Cami sighed.

Why are you worried? French was one of Cami's strong points, for all that her tongue used to trip over every syllable. Sister Mary Brefoil didn't call on her, one of the few real instances of mercy Ruby had ever seen in a classroom. "This is just so useless. Why the hell is a past participle even *necessary?*"

"Diplomacy." Ellie brushed her pale hair back, glancing up at the overhead fixture. The hum of conversation surrounding them wasn't quite mutinous, but it was close. "There's practical applications too."

"It was a rhetorical question." At least they were off the subject of how Ruby *felt*.

Cami dropped her schoolbag and opened her notebook. "Want to come over? Spend the night?"

"Sure." Ellie's acceptance was casual, almost rehearsed. So they were planning a get-together.

"Ruby?" Cami looked downright hopeful. She'd taken to pulling her hair back, and the architecture of her face, clearly revealed, was beautiful enough to send a pang through just about anyone.

"Can't." Ruby hunched her shoulders. "Got a houseguest."

"You can't even . . ." Cami hushed as Sister Mary sailed in through the door, round and bouncy, her apple cheeks flushed and her rosary swinging. "Can you come to dinner, then?"

"Have to ask Gran." Why bother, when she knew the answer? She was supposed to be keeping Conrad happy, and that meant staying home. He didn't want to go anywhere unless it was just the two of them, and he wanted to drive. She wasn't about to sit in her car and let someone else steer, so she found reasons not to.

Ellie finally broke down and asked. "Any news?"

Meaning, *about Hunter?*

Ruby shook her head.

"Bonjour, mademoiselles!" Sister Mary picked up the yard-stick laid precisely across her ruthlessly organized desk. Last year someone had pranked her inkwell; now *that* had been an occasion.

"Bonjour, Sœur Marie," they dutifully chorused.

The Sister beamed, always a bad sign. *"Vous êtes très chanceux. Il s'agit d'un quiz aujourd'hui!"*

Ruby worked the words around in her head. Great. The suppressed groans going around the room were probably food for Sister Mary, who tapped her yardstick briskly against the desk and turned to the chalkboard.

A piece of paper slid into Ruby's peripheral vision. Ellie's handwriting, fast and graceful like the rest of her.

Would it help if we asked Gran for you?

Ruby shook her head and concentrated on the Sister's scratchy voice rising through a question. Chalk scratched against the board, her neck itched, and she had to blink several times before the welling in her eyes went away.

She was going to bomb it anyway, so why even try? Still, it was better than seeing Ellie's concerned expression. Cami kept peeking around Ellie, too, trying to see Ruby's face.

They were worried.

Buck up, Ruby. Be what they need. She took a deep breath, stared down at her paper, and started translating. For the rest of the day, she was going to have to be cheerful. Again.

FIFTEEN

IT WAS A RELIEF TO GET HOME. THE GARDEN SWEL-tered under a gray-lensed sky, Gran's blueberry bushes holding wizened late fruit under leaves beginning to dapple with fall colors. Every crack in the slate path was familiar, every bush an old friend; the rampion had bolted and so had the radishes. Even the silvery rue looked happy to see her, and it didn't ask any questions.

Inside, the charmed coolness was a balm. She slung her schoolbag onto the counter, opened the fridge, and found a bottle of fresh-pressed apple juice.

Somehow Gran always knew when it was time for apples. The only question was whether she should pour a glass or just drink straight from the—

"Hello, Ruby."

She almost dropped the bottle, slammed the fridge door. "Christ. I didn't hear you." He was *quiet*, even for kin. Her heart hammered, the fridge's compressor humming to itself under its layer of sealcharm. She hadn't smelled him, but then, she hadn't been trying to, and he'd lived here for more than a couple days.

Conrad leaned against the doorway to the living room. The lights were off, cloud-screened sunshine gleaming off the copper-bottomed pans in their rack over the range. In the almost-gloom, his eyes were chips of amber, and he looked solemn. He hadn't shaved. The scruffiness was kind of appealing.

"Hi. I thought you were out driving." *Driving my car, that is.*

He shrugged. Why was he looking at her so intently?

Well, now she had to get a glass down. She couldn't just slog off the bottle. "How was your day?"

"Fine." He kept watching her.

"You want some?" She sloshed the juice a little, tried a smile. "It's not honeywine, but it'll do."

"No."

He wasn't exactly chatty today. That suited her just fine, actually, so she poured herself a glass and was contemplating some toast to get her through homework when he spoke in her ear.

"Ruby."

She jumped again, almost knocking the bottle over. How was he so damn *silent*? She could hear everyone else, even Gran. "Quit *doing* that!" He was way too close, shoving her against the counter, and a bright dart of unfamiliar fear went through her.

A red scent was all over him. Coppery, old, crusted, it lurked under kinsmell and scraped against her nerves. Her skin rippled with the precursors to the shift, sweat springing out in pinpoint prickledrops. Her skirt swung, and the glass of apple juice top-pled, sticky and cold.

Great, I'm going to have to clean that up—

"Brett called," he said, pleasantly, in her ear. His breath was too warm, he grabbed her wrist and squeezed a little. "Anything you want to tell me, *Rube?*"

Brett? The boytoy, he had the number to her bedroom phone. She'd forgotten all about that. *What the hell?* The juice was soaking into her shirt, the counter cutting into her belly. "Get *off* me."

His fingers clamped down on her wrist. Small bones ground together; she half-screamed. "*Ow!* What's *wrong* with you?"

"Is he kin? This Brett?"

"What? No! He's just—" *Just a mere-human.* What would *that* sound like, to him? She couldn't get a breath in right, and her head started ringing. That awful roaring sound had just been waiting to jump on her again. "Just a *friend!*"

"He sounded pretty friendly, all right." Another hard squeeze, grinding her wrist.

"*Ow!*" The roaring in her head intensified. "Stop it!"

"So should I go somewhere else, huh? You've got someone lined up already? Some little pink punk?"

Is that what he thinks? "What? No, he's just—*ow!* He's just a friend! Stop it!" The words spiraled up into a breathless squeal. "Please. *It's not what you think Conrad please!*"

He let go of her, all at once. Ruby whirled and backed up sideways along the counter, her shirt soaking up cold apple juice along the back too. Her skirt's waistband, wet clear through, rasped against her skin. She rubbed her wrist and stared at him.

Narrowed eyes, still glowing-hot. His hair tumbled as if he'd just run his hands back through it, or as if he'd been roughhousing. Was this what Grimtree cousins did? Some of the boykin liked horseplay, but they never . . . never . . .

She couldn't even think, the roaring swallowed everything inside her head.

His face changed, as if he was about to shift. He stepped toward her, and Ruby flinched, scooting away along the sink.

"God. Ruby." Harshly, dry. "I . . . I'm sorry. I just . . . you're so . . . you're beautiful. And I'm just . . . I thought you'd . . ." His ribs heaved, deep flaring breaths. Heavy musk in the kitchen, both of them were sweating. Hot water on her cheeks, and curls knocked loose over her face.

You thought I what? She swallowed, hard. "You hurt my wrist." Flat and toneless, someone else using her voice again. Who?

Did she want to know?

"I'm sorry." He took another step. This time she didn't flinch, just pulled her wrist close to her chest and stared at him. "I don't . . . I just don't want to lose you."

Their combined smell, along with the roaring, made it difficult to think, difficult to *breathe*. The shift was close to the surface; she pushed it down. If Gran found out . . . what would she think? If she walked into the kitchen right now and smelled this, she might think that Ruby and Conrad had . . . had . . . done something *else*. Something irrevocable.

Would she be disappointed? Or would she start making marriage noises? Moving the betrothal up a notch. Mithrus knew the clan needed something to take its mind off Hunter dead in the Park.

"I have to clean this up." She couldn't make it any louder than a whisper. Her throat was a pinhole. Her skin ran with pins and needles, and a high brassy edge of fear had invaded her scent. "Gran'll be home soon."

He stared at her like she'd just started speaking a foreign language. Had she said it in French? She didn't think so. Her wrist throbbed, her cheeks flamed, and the fridge clicked into life, making its familiar low hum. Potential sparked once, twice in the space between them—the edge of Ruby's personal space flexing. She wasn't as high-powered as Ellie, but she had more than *him*, that was for sure. His Potential was merely a low umber glow, rasping against hers before retreating.

Conrad whirled and vanished into the living room. A few seconds later the front door slammed, and now he was making noise. He ran down the slate path like the Wild Hunt was after him.

Kin

Ruby shut her eyes, cradling her wrist, and sagged against the counter. The roaring inside her head crested again, but this time she welcomed it. She didn't want to think about what had just happened.

What did *just happen?* Her wrist throbbed, ached. *Mithrus Christ, what was that?*

SIXTEEN

GRAN'S GUMBO WAS JUST ABOUT THE BEST THING IN the world. Spicy, smoky, hot and wonderful, ladled over imported rice and with a slice of Dalkenna Grocer's crusty bread, sending up steam in fragrant whorls and burning comfortably in your stomach while you washed the dishes afterward—she'd eaten it all her life, and there was almost nothing better.

Tonight, though, she just picked at a prawn drenched with savory broth. "He was gone when I came home." It wasn't exactly lying, she told herself. It was *protecting*.

Gran set the bread down. She wore the crimson housedress today, her hair rebraided and the smell of violets from her soap wafting around her. "He didn't leave a note?"

Ruby shrugged. Her wrist throbbed, maroon and dark-blue bruising rising to the surface, but she'd wrapped a couple hemp bracelets around it like she sometimes did. You couldn't see the worst of it, and Gran wasn't looking. "No."

Kin

You weren't really supposed to charm outside school, but she'd thrown a couple air-cleaning ones around, popping them off her fingers just like Ellie. Her first instinct—to spill the whole story to Gran—ran up against the wall of what Conrad might say in return. Brett was Berch Prep, which was fine, but he was also mere-human, and if Gran took to asking questions, well, some of Ruby's nighttime party prowls might come to light.

That was a prospect to give her a chill or two. Keeping her mouth shut was the best policy. Even if she was just protecting her own sorry hide.

I don't want to lose you. Was it that important to him?

Was *she* that important? Now she could see, kind of, why he got mad. If he didn't want to go home, or if he really planned on going into the Waste if she didn't like him . . . she could sort of see it.

Still, her wrist hurt. Her chest hurt. Hungry as she was, the gumbo just didn't want to go down. If she hunched over her bowl, she'd get a *Sit up, please . . . Ruby? Are you unwell?*

Gran settled in her own high-backed chair with a sigh. "I confess I'm glad to have a moment with you. I've missed our time together."

That helped, and didn't help, at the same time. Her chest eased a little, but there were all sorts of things Gran could disapprove of lurking in every corner. Time alone with her was likely to be yet another minefield to dance through. "Me too."

The old woman broke a crusty bit of bread, looked down at her bowl. "How was school today?"

"French quiz. Think I bombed it."

"It is a difficult language, sometimes." Crunch of breaking crust, splash of spoon. Ruby sipped at a little broth, swallowed hard. "Your friends. Camille, and Ellen. How are they?"

What is this? She darted a look up, but Gran was frowning slightly into her gumbo. "They're okay. Cami's Potential settled."

"Ah. Is there a celebration?"

I don't know. "Maybe, I don't know yet."

Silence. "You have been doing your chores with great alacrity lately." Did Gran sound, of all things, *tentative*?

"Trying."

"And Conrad? Does he help?"

Ruby watched her gumbo, drawing a spoon through it as if admiring the colors. "He's a guest. I don't let him."

Gran nodded, thoughtfully. "The Grimtree seem to have different manners."

"I noticed." *That's one word for it.* She scooped up a mouthful of rice. She *had* to eat, Gran would notice if she didn't. There would be questions. Her wrist throbbed insistently.

"Very different manners indeed. Ruby . . ." Gran paused, forged on. "Do you like him?"

So *that* was what she was aiming at.

What did Gran expect her to say? *No, send him home?* Or

even, *Yeah, but not enough?* What was enough? She owed the clan, and he liked her.

Enough to get jealous. *I don't want to lose you.*

"He's okay." That sounded unhelpful. What else could she say? "I'm trying, Gran. Really I am."

"I know. I see you trying, and I . . ." Gran broke the bread into smaller and smaller pieces, dusting them into her bowl. "Sometimes you remind me of . . ."

Ruby splashed her spoon a little, as if she were five again. Of course, back then she hadn't ever worried about who she reminded Gran of.

But she had padded down the hall almost every night to see if Gran was breathing. Sometimes she'd even hidden under Gran's big heirloom bed and slept there, until Gran waited one night to catch her and say *you might as well come in, child.* There, next to the safety and warmth keeping all nightly terrors away, Ruby could sleep.

She'd stopped doing that when she was about ten, but sometimes she wished she was five again.

Ruby cocked her head, and her heart began to pound. Gran caught the sound as well, and frowned, slightly.

The front door opened. Footsteps. What was he going to say?

Conrad stepped into the kitchen, his black hair slicked down. His boots were wet, but he'd wiped them carefully. It looked like he'd run through a sprinkler or something, and he was redolent of sap and crushed grass. "Did I miss dinner? I'm sorry. It smells fantastic."

Gran pushed her chair back, but Ruby was already on her feet to get him a bowl of rice and gumbo. And also, to stand on tiptoe to get down a charmcrystal vase for the wet daisies he carried, holding them awkwardly in one fist, his expression rueful and hopeful at once as he stepped carefully across the kitchen toward her. "I brought these. For you."

Why was she so relieved? "Thank you." Inside her ribs, a tightness eased, and she found out she was hungry after all.

SEVENTEEN

SHE SAT ON THE FRONT STEP, HUGGING HER BARE
knees as thunder rolled in the distance. Autumn storms would
start coming in soon, but for right now it was sticky and the
sky-bowling was just a heavenly headache. Out over the Waste
it might be raining somewhere, Tesla's Folly crackling between
earth and sky, lighting up the twisted ruins of a world mere-
humans used to own.

Who owned it now? Maybe the Waste did, and it saw the
cities and kolkhozes as intrusions. A planetary cancer.

The top band of her shorts dug into the slight rash her sod-
den skirt had worn around her waist. Sometimes she stretched
out her hurt wrist, rotating it, wincing a little each time a sharp
jab of pain speared though. The swelling wasn't bad, and kin
healed quickly. It would be fine tomorrow morning, most
likely. Still, it hurt.

He came out quietly, his boots creaking a little. Sank down

beside her, a different heat than the breathless mugginess. She rested her chin on her knees, heels braced against the step and her toes bare and vulnerable in the hot humidity.

They sat like that, while the thunder-train rolled on greased wheels overhead.

When the sound had died, he moved slightly.

Ruby flinched.

He put his hand back down. "I'm sorry."

Me too. She stared at the garden's far wall, a low stone affair. Everyone who could afford it walled their house off, a leftover from the days just after the Reeve. Maybe Gran was saying, *Go ahead, come and get me.* Or maybe she just didn't care. It wasn't likely that she'd ever been scared.

What was it like, to be fearless? If you weren't born that way, could you learn it?

"If you want, I'll go." Conrad leaned forward, bracing his elbows on his knees. "I, uh. I've never been what anyone's wanted. I just thought . . . I'm not what you want, either."

You don't know what I want. "You hurt me." The words were toneless. It was the best she could do. She didn't want to sound accusing, but . . .

Exactly. But.

He made a short, exhaled sound, as if he'd been hit in the stomach. "I'm sorry. I don't want to. I just . . . I thought you . . . you're so beautiful, and I'm just . . ."

134

Kin

"Just what?" All the same, a traitorous spot of heat bloomed deep inside her. He thought she was beautiful.

"I don't know." Almost angry, but maybe it could have been because he had to raise his voice over the distant thunder. "I thought, well, why would you want *me* around? I'm just another way they're trying to cage you."

Which probably made them even. "And I guess I'm just another way they're trying to cage *you*."

"Nah." His head dropped.

The steaming city under a lid of cloud rumbled uneasily, again. When she was little she used to think it was the core making that noise. Just like a big dozing animal, crouched in the center of New Haven and groaning under its own weight of curdled, clotted Potential.

"How is it different?" She watched the sky fluoresce, breathing in the heat. Her T-shirt was getting sticky, and she had a scab on her knee from hitting the cupboard that afternoon while he had . . . hurt her.

"You're my way *out* of a cage." He said it to the flagstone walk, as if he expected her to laugh at him. "You don't know. You just don't know."

"I guess I don't." The scab on her knee was rough and fresh, still smarting.

"I didn't mean to hurt you."

"I know." *Do I?* There were the daisies in their vase, safe on the kitchen table. The way he'd looked when he offered them, though Gran sort of sniffed when he sat down all wet to dinner.

The way he'd looked horrified and run away. Maybe he hadn't really meant to . . . do what he did.

"Do you want me to go?" He said it so softly she almost didn't hear.

Ruby hesitated, between yes and no, for a long time. So long, in fact, that he spoke again.

"You asked about . . . my brother. He's . . . he was everything they wanted. He got everything first, and best, and always. No matter how hard I tried, I couldn't . . . I think I did this to get away from him. I loved him, but . . . there's just only so much you can take."

Don't I know it. Only Ruby didn't have a sister, even though a single girlchild wasn't treated the same as a boy-only. A living, breathing sister Rube could have fought with, relied on. She had Cami and Ellie, but it wasn't the same. They were moving on, growing up.

No sister. No mother, either. Just a ghost she was measured against. The person she reminded Gran of, the one never spoken of. You couldn't fight with a ghost, or prank it, or find a way around it.

You could only be *less*. Ghosts didn't make mistakes, they didn't criticize or act up or bomb a French quiz. They weren't selfish. They were *perfect*. Even hating them brought no relief.

She uncurled slowly. Put her bare feet on the walk. Gritty

slate under her feet, slightly damp and blood-warm. Her pale, vulnerable toes, and his thick heavy boots.

"Don't go," she said, finally. "Please."

"You mean it?" Soft and wondering. He reached over, slowly, as if expecting her to flinch again, and touched her shoulder with two fingertips. Gently, so gently.

A dark, secret thrill poured through her. The heat outside her skin wasn't so bad, compared to the glow that lit itself inside her chest and belly and legs. "Of course I do. Just . . . don't do that again, okay?"

He nodded, half-seen in the dusk. A glimmer of those golden eyes. Whatever reply he would have made was lost in the sound of running feet.

Thorne bolted through the gate, wild-haired and wide-eyed. "Ruby!" He skidded to a stop, and didn't hit Conrad by a sheer miracle. The Grimtree was on his feet, facing down Thorne, who leapt aside and almost knocked over a terracotta pot full of strawberry plants. "The Clanmother. We need her."

She found herself on her feet too. Conrad, tense and a little sheepish, slowly lowered his hands. Did he think Thorne was going to jump them? "What happened?"

"It's . . . the Park." His sides flickered with deep starving breaths, and the words came out in hard heaves. "There's been . . . another murder."

• • •

"Oncle just said to come get you." Thorne, still breathless, braced a hand against the hallway wall and hunched his shoulders. "There's cops."

Gran's pale eyebrow raised as she settled her purse on her shoulder. "Police?"

"It's not kin." Thorne glanced at Ruby, who stood, hugging herself, charmcooled air brushing her bare legs. "Mere-human. Girl."

"You should go upstairs." Conrad, right next to her, was a tall warm bulk. He probably didn't mean to loom like that, but she had to admit it was sort of comforting.

"How bad is it?" Gran was already halfway across the living room, heading for the massive mahogany charmer's hutch. The tapestry made little skritching sounds as the threads shifted, and Conrad looked at it like he expected it to start speaking. The charmer's sun-and-moon were veiled, the Moon's smile sad and worried, the stars around them tarnished.

Thorne glanced at Ruby, straightened. High, wild color stood out in his cheeks, and the sweat on him glistened. His T-shirt was stuck to his back, and muscle flickered under its thin screen. "Pretty bad. Clanmother . . . it's like him."

"Him?" Gran paused.

"Like . . ." He glanced at Ruby, plunged ahead. "Like Hunt."

Ruby swayed. Her shoulder hit Conrad's. *Oh, God.* "No," she whispered.

A heavy arm around her shoulders. Conrad pulled a little, and she let him steer her. The roaring in her head tried to come back; she pushed it away.

"I see." Gran shook her head, her mouth turning down. She stepped into a pair of flats, and she was apparently planning on leaving the cottage in her housedress. "How many police?"

"Six. They came to Oncle Efraim's door, said they don't want an incident. There's a detective—Haelan. He asked for you personally, Oncle told me to run."

"Haelan." Gran's teeth, sharp and white, showed in a swift grimace. No kin liked the police. "You've done well, Thorne. Conrad, my apologies, I must attend to this. Ruby, is your homework done?"

There's a dead body and you're asking about my homework? "Can I come with you?" *Don't leave me here alone.*

Well, technically not alone, but . . . the roaring kept wanting to come back. It was hard to think through it.

A single shake of her pale head; Gran checked her purse, frowning slightly. "Of course not. It's a school night. Go to bed and don't worry. Thorne, please wait in the hall. I shall be out directly."

"She's old enough," he said, instead of hopping to obey. "And she'll be Clanmother one day."

Gran halted. She turned slowly to face Thorne, who had drawn himself up. Under the wild thatch of wheat-colored hair, dark eyes glinting, his chin up in that same defiant tilt . . . Ruby let out a soft sipping breath.

He looked sharply handsome, almost Wild. And incredibly, painfully rebellious.

The old woman simply examined him from top to toe. "Indeed she will," she finally agreed, "but for right now, she is still a child, and so are you. Your elders will deal with this, whatever it is, so that you may have your childhood a little while longer. Go into the hall, young one."

Ruby closed her eyes. Conrad's arm tightened. "Don't worry." He probably meant to say it softly. "It'll be all right." He drew her up the stairs, away from all of it, and she let him.

Thorne didn't wait in the hall. Instead, the front door slammed, and he was gone as quickly as he'd shown up, out into the gathering storm.

EIGHTEEN

Impossible to sleep, even though the cooling charms in each room were refreshed and actively humming. Thunder muttered in the Waste, a dozing creature wrapped around the city walls.

Ruby finally rolled out of bed and wandered to the bathroom, then downstairs. The sky-grumbles only added to the silence of past midnight, underscoring the quiet. The light in the kitchen was on, a warm golden glow of buffered glass incandescents.

Gran was at the table, again, dark smudges under her eyes. She did not glance at Ruby, staring at the playing cards as she shuffled them again. Her hair was tangled into its nightly braid and spilled down her back as a pale rope. Her fingers flicked, laying out the cards in a wheel-pattern instead of her usual five up-and-down.

Sometimes at night they didn't talk to each other, Ruby just got a drink or a snack and went back upstairs. Tonight, though,

Ruby sat down in her usual spot, brushing curls out of her face.

The cards blurred as she blinked and rubbed at grainy sleepsand.

Tesla's Folly kept sparking. It was enough to make you wish for rain, for screaming, for broken glass. Anything to break the tension.

"You're worried," she said, finally, folding her arms on the table, laying her head down on them as if she was in primary school and bored. Her deportment grades had never been above passable, ever.

Maybe she should have tried harder from the beginning.

Gran didn't reply for a long moment. Then she nodded. "Yes."

"Is someone hunting us?" *Or just killing in the Park? Trying to make us seem like . . . like what?* "Or trying to frighten us? Or . . ."

"Je ne sais pas, ma belle." Gran turned over a jack, another, both red. Blots of color from Ruby's perspective, the table-edge a distant infinity. "This is a troubled time, indeed."

I've been trying to make it less troubled. "I'm sorry."

A ghost of a smile touched Gran's thin lips. "You are a relief instead of a burden, little one."

She hasn't called me that in ages. She watched Gran's hands, familiar and bone-pale, unpainted nails short but nicely buffed and trimmed. No age spots; there were charms for that. *My vanity,* Gran would remark occasionally, *will overwhelm me one day, no doubt.*

"I'm trying." Now that she could hear Gran's breathing, smell the comforting musk and whiff of Levarin perfume that meant safety, her eyelids were heavy. The kitchen was restored to order after gumbo, except for a water glass set by the toaster—Conrad's. Cheerful tomato-red fridge, the red counters wiped and the floor swept clean with a mopcharm, and except for that one lone glass Ruby could pretend it was just them again.

And except for her wrist, tucked out of sight. It still ached a little.

"You try so hard, Ruby." Now Gran glanced at her, a penetrating look. Her irises were steel-colored again, and any of the cousins might have quailed under that gaze. But Gran was just thoughtful, not severe, though if you didn't live with her you might mistake one for the other. "Sometimes I think you try too hard."

The thump below Ruby's breastbone must have shown on her face, because Gran shook her head, slightly. "No, I don't mean it that way. I meant only that I fear you may do yourself some harm, seeking to fill ..." She halted, as if groping for words. "You are not alone. The clan confines, but it also protects."

Like a straitener's jacket, right? So I can't hurt myself or anyone else.

Like a collar. "Gran ..."

It was maybe Gran's turn to wonder what Ruby might say. *Don't collar me?* Or even, *I'm scared.* Keeping everything whirling was a full-time job, and now it felt like it was going to speed up even further. All the fast driving in the world couldn't outrun this.

A girl was dead in the Park. Just like Hunter. Who would *do* something like that?

"I made many . . . mistakes, with your mother." Gran's hands now lay against the cards, their white and red and black quivering uneasily. "I . . . do not ever want to repeat them, with you. I am trying too." A slight smile, again. "In all senses of the word, I expect."

There was a prickling behind her eyes. Hot and heavy, and she denied it. "I love you," Ruby whispered. "You're not bad at all, Gran."

Well, that was damning with faint praise. But Gran's smile widened a trifle, and just for a moment everything between them eased. Thunder rumbled again, but farther away. Some storms were like that. They flirted, they teased, until you just wanted to explode.

Was this what a boytoy felt like when Ruby did the same? That was an uncomfortable thought, and she was having a lot of them lately. Was that what adulthood did to you, fill your head with everything you'd rather not think about?

How could you *not* think about the whispers in the corners, the half-heard words? She'd heard them as she lay upstairs, stiff as a poker in her bed. The girl had been found splayed out in a glade within sight of the road, torn open.

Savaged. Torn. Blood. The marks. Hushed voices as Oncles

and Tantes consulted the Clanmother, Gran's replies quiet and pointed. She was so calm.

"I love you, too, child. You are very far from bad." Gran gathered the cards. "Do you want some warm milk? It will help you sleep."

"Nah. I'd have to brush my teeth again." Ruby hunched, stretching her back, then extended her bare toes under the table, pointing them as if she were back at Madame Vole's Dance Academy. Ballet was finicky, there was no space in it for exuberance, but it was the dance you were supposed to learn if you were part of New Haven's upper crust. Of course Cami floated right through it, and Ellie was as precise and gliding as always. Ruby was always putting her limbs in the wrong place, too much expression, too much fidgeting, *slow down.* "It's really bad, isn't it. The . . . in the Park."

Gran rose, slowly, pushing her chair back. "You have enough to worry about. *That* is mine to solve."

But if I'm going to be Clanmother . . . well, it wasn't certain that she *would* be, was it, now? "Okay." She tried not to sound dubious.

"I am not so fragile yet that I need children to shoulder my responsibilities. You have much of your youth left; I wish for you to . . . to *have* it."

Which was an awfully nice idea, but there were all sorts of things in the way. One of them was sleeping upstairs, and her wrist twinged just a little. "It's okay, Gran."

Edalie nodded and shuffled for the fridge. Her embroidered slippers made their peculiar sound, light and deliberate, as unique as Gran herself.

The words crowding in Ruby's throat wouldn't help anything. Sending Conrad back and handling negotiations for another prospect to visit would be just another drain on Gran's time and energy, and the last thing she needed was Ruby whining at her.

Especially with murders in Woodsdowne Park. Ruby hid the shudder by stretching and yawning. "I'm going to bed. School tomorrow."

"Dream well, child."

"I'll try." *Though I don't think it's very likely.*

The stairs creaked in their old familiar voices, and she halted halfway up, cocking her head. Had she heard a quiet snick, the guest room door closing so, so softly? Or a brush of feet against the hall carpet?

Nothing else, and of course the hall was starting to hold threads of Conrad's smoke and musk under the blankets of other familiar scents that were her-and-Gran. Maybe he'd wanted to come downstairs, or she was just hearing the cottage creak even though the nights weren't cooling off. New Haven was under a dome of nasty expectant weather, and it would only get thicker until a storm could come in.

It was there, standing stock-still, that she realized the cards hadn't been quivering because of Potential. No, Gran's hands had been shaking, just a little. Which gave Ruby such a weird, unsettled feeling in her stomach she ran softly up the remaining stairs and into her room, as if a childhood monster was right behind her.

NINETEEN

LOCKERS SLAMMING, CATCALLS BRIGHT PIERCING notes over conversation surf-noise, high-pitched laughter echoing against the high ceilings. Ruby stared into the depths of her locker, neatly arranged this early in the year, and blinked several times, trying to think of what she should grab. What came next?

"*There* you are." Ellie reached past her, slid the French book out, and flipped open Ruby's bag. "You need this. And this. Got a notebook?"

"I think so." Ruby blinked. Ellie was already digging in her red canvas schoolbag, almost yanking it off Ruby's shoulder. "Ell, relax. I've got a notebook."

Ellie shook her pale hair back, blowing irritably at a single, slightly waving strand. "You're dead on your feet. Come on, we're going to be late. Cami's holding our pew."

"Can't we just skip it?" She knew the answer before she even said it, and for once, was too damn tired to care. "It's just a bunch of singing and listening to homilies."

"Now *there's* the Ruby I know. We missed you at Babchat last night."

"Trouble."

"We figured. Cami heard from Nico."

"Of course he'd hear. Why would he bother her with it, though?" Ruby slammed her locker shut with a vengeance. "He's a piece of work."

Ellie paused for a moment, eyeing her as a wave of Year 10s flooded the hall. They had chapel earlier than everyone else. Maybe some of them even took it seriously. Bright-eyed, dew-cheeked, and smooth-haired in the blue wool blazer and ubiquitous plaid skirt, they all looked the same. It took getting a whiff to tell them apart.

Either that or a closer look than Ruby cared to give. It was all the same, anyway. This year thin headbands were out and hair ribbons were in, the luckcharms on their polished mary-janes were bugle-shaped silver beads instead of the flat sharp-edged dangles they'd been last year, and jangling feyweight bracelets were making a comeback.

I haven't worn a feyweight since Year Eight. The little clip-on figures were the hottest thing going for three years running, hard to find and spawning thousands of cheap knockoffs. Even a ban by the City Council hadn't stopped kids from wearing them, though it had driven import profits up into the stratosphere. Gran had even given her a few handfuls of the little things, smiling a peculiar little grimace.

Ruby's old pair of feyweight bracelets—one for each wrist, because of course that was the thing to aim for—was probably in a jumble in the bottom of the rosewood box atop her dresser. She'd scored clip-on jangles for Ellie and Cami too, the three of them walking in a sphere of laughter and chiming through Havenvale Middle School.

Everything used to be so simple.

"She's worried about you." Gray eyes paler than Gran's, Ellie's expression was a watered-down version of the concern sometimes drawing down Gran's face whenever Ruby had done or said something too careless. "You don't Babchat, you don't come over, you don't talk about anything, you know, real. We miss you."

Maybe Cami might, but you probably don't. I'm a selfish bitch, remember? "Just been busy, you know, with everything going on." Ruby spun her locker's dial, the identicharm on it flushing red briefly as it sealed itself. "Let's get to chapel."

"Ruby." Ellie didn't give up easily, gliding next to her as Ruby set off for chapel at a good clip, swimming against the hallway-current. "Look, ever since Hunter—"

Oh, hell no. "I don't want to talk about it. Is that okay with you?" A little *too* aggressive, but if she had to start unpacking the details right here she might as well just run away screaming.

Come to think of it, the idea had its merits. Just run and run, get to the Semprena—hooray for Conrad *letting* her drive her own car again. . . .

Dammit. She didn't want to think about him. Conrad had eaten dinner while she cleaned up the kitchen last night. Maybe he was hungry; he put away two bowls of gumbo, complimenting Gran's cooking. He could have been trying to keep her mind off things, or just nervously talking.

Her wrist twinged a bit, only when she torqued it the wrong way. She could still feel his breath on her ear, warm and dangerous. And see his boots next to her bare toes, while he told her something he probably hadn't told a single other person.

Something to hold, just between the two of them. Shiny and fragile like spun charmglass. Just like Gran, later at the table.

Ellie caught her arm. "I was just asking. You know, if you want to talk. We're good for that, you know. Both of us."

So good at talking you never told me what the hell was going on with either of you. So it was Ruby's turn to keep a secret or two from them, stuff it into that little place inside her where other confidences glowed.

Luckily, Ruby's secrets weren't dangerous. Just stupid stuff about growing up, that was all. It was selfish of her to even *act* like she had a problem.

All harmless things, except for one. Had Hunter been hoping she'd go out on one of her nightly prowls?

Gran was going to be home late and headed into the office early too. Even if she wasn't, there wasn't a whole lot she'd tell Ruby. The radio news this morning, while she sat alone in the Semprena because Cami had taken to picking Ellie up on her way to school, didn't have much either. The murdered girl was from Hollow Hills, a scholarship student, law enforcement had no comment and asked for the family's privacy to be considered.

How long would *that* last? The tabloids were going to have a field day. And of course, there would be whispers.

About Woodsdowne.

The chapel doors loomed in front of them, old dark wood worked with Mithrus's *tau* cross and bull horns, the Magdalen's sad eyes carved around them and rubbed with a stain that once had been bright crimson but now was a deep ochre. Like painted bones.

"It's okay," Ruby said, finally. Ellie kept gliding next to her, her arm through Ruby's as if they were younger and gossiping instead of older and lonely, walking side by side with their physical proximity hiding a distance greater than the Waste.

Inside. Where it didn't show.

"It doesn't *sound* okay." Ellie's fingers tightened, just a little. "But when you want to, you know, talk, I'm here. Okay?"

They weren't quite late, the organ was softly noodling under a rustling of bored Year 12 girls nevertheless glad of something that wasn't class time. Cami was still standing, her long inky hair straight as a ruler, holding their usual bench. Uneasy Potential sparked and flirted along the wooden backs, despite the layer upon layer of suppressive charm meant to make sure the girls didn't prank each other—or the teachers—into oblivion.

"I'll keep it in mind," Ruby muttered. "Come on."

Kin

Binksy Malone, blonde hair shining in the gentle golden light, elbowed one of her coterie and jerked a chin at Ruby. They both giggled, and it was middle school all over again. Except then, Ruby would have snarled.

Ellie's eyes narrowed, and her fingers flicked along her other side, hidden from the Sisters up on the dais and in the gallery. There was a sharp crackle, lost in the rest of the sound, and Binksy's perfectly manicured hand flew up to her mouth.

Good. I hope that stung.

"Didn't know you could throw a popcharm that far," Ruby whispered, keeping her lips still as the organ music petered out. Ancient Sister Alice Angels-Abiding, the music teacher, shuffled yellowed hymn-sheet pages and glanced over the chapel's gloomy interior. *Especially under the dampers. Wow.*

"If she doesn't shut up I'll hex her hair off," was Ellie's muttered reply.

"Come on." Cami motioned them into the bench, and when Mother Heloise, the principal and prime potentate of St. Juno's, turned her beneficent round-faced smile upon the massed girls, Ellie was grinning broadly.

Ruby tried to smile, her face a cracked, unfamiliar mask. All through chapel, there was warmth on either side of her, Cami still and straight-backed, Ellie leaning against Ruby whenever they were seated.

How selfish was it, then, that Ruby still felt so cold?

TWENTY

HIGH CHARM CALC HOMEWORK WAS A BITCH TO DO on your own. Instead of curling up on her bed to do it, or tapping at her Babbage, she liked to spread it out on the kitchen table. Unfortunately, the breathless heat outside was creeping into the house, despite layers of coolcharming. Gran had even left a note that Ruby could refresh the coolcharms herself, despite the prohibition against Juno girls with unsettled Potential charming without supervision.

Which still wouldn't have been so bad if Conrad hadn't been hovering, his golden irises glittering. "Let's go to the Park. You can do that later."

"Gran expects me to keep my grades up." She tried to concentrate, wrote the equation on a fresh piece of paper. The trouble was you never knew which ones were unsolvable if your Potential hadn't settled, so you had to work each one at least twice before you could mark it correctly. Ell was a whiz at

High Charm Calc, but without her on Babbage Ruby was left to her own devices.

At least it gave her brain something to focus on other than bodies in the Park.

"Come on. Don't you want to have some fun?" Cajoling. He leaned against the counter, cloudy sunlight on his broad shoulders. If he just left her alone for a little while she could get this *done*.

"Looking for dead bodies does not sound *fun*. It sounds *gruesome*." She worked the equation again, frowned as it came out the same. Made a notation on the worksheet, moved on to the next.

"I don't want to look for dead bodies. I want to roam with you." His hands worked against each other, knuckles cracking as the shift blurred and rippled under his skin. Ruby hunched her shoulders.

"Maybe after I finish this. But you have to let me finish."

"Am I distracting you, schoolgirl?" He probably didn't mean it to sound so dismissive. It was *schoolgirl* when she refused him something, and *kingirl* when she didn't. "Maybe I should just leave."

Which way was she supposed to take *that*? Ruby put her head down a little farther, feeling his hot gaze on her. Was he angry? "You could just let me finish this."

The smoke in his scent was maybe anger. She took a deep

breath, trying to ignore the shift prickling under her own skin in response. Her skirt left her legs bare, but it was Juno wool, scratchy against the back of her thighs. Her blazer, draped over the back of the chair, held heat like a sponge even when she was only near it.

Whatever Conrad was going to say was interrupted by a tinkling charmbell. After that, three quick raps, and Ruby's heart leapt with relief. She was on her feet and across the kitchen in a heartbeat, and the front door opened to reveal Thorne, his wheat hair a mess, a black tank top and the well-worn paint-splattered jeans he wore after school hugging his legs.

"Boo." He slid in quickly, she slammed the door and popped a refresh of the nearest coolcharm off her fingers, snapping it right next to him so he'd feel a puff of fresh air. "Thanks."

"Is it bad news?" She crossed her arms, fresh worry exploding in her stomach. "Gran's at the office, so—"

"Nope." He grinned, a wide white wolfish expression. "Just came to see you, pretty girl."

Her own smile didn't feel like a cracked mask now. "There's iced tea in the fridge. Unsweetened, the kind you like."

"Aren't you hospitable." It was meant kindly, but nobody else would have known. He raked his fingers back through his hair and followed her toward the kitchen. "The Grimtree here?"

"If you're not rude, you can hang out with him while I finish my homework. High Charm Calc, I've got to get it done."

Kin

"Sure. I'll be polite as fuck."

Her giggle cut off halfway as she stepped back into the kitchen. Conrad's face was unreadable, and the smoky scent was stronger than ever.

"Thorne's here. You remember him, right? You guys can hang out while I finish, and we can go rambling together."

"Afternoon." Thorne's tone was neutral, and he headed for the fridge. "How are you liking New Haven, cousin?"

"Some parts are pretty." Conrad's chin lifted. "Others, not so much."

"Same as everywhere." Thorne grabbed a glass, turned to the fridge. "Let's head to the living room. Give Rube some quiet so she can finish, and then we can have some fun."

"I don't think so." Pleasant, but cold. "I'm going upstairs. Have fun without me. You probably will."

Ruby almost gasped. Conrad headed straight for her, and she had to step aside or be knocked over. He gave her one cutting glance, then was gone. The stairs shuddered and the guest room door slammed behind him, rattling the entire cottage.

Thorne, standing in front of the open fridge, actually gaped. It wasn't often that he looked stunned. He left the iced tea in there, and swung it shut. "I was *perfectly* polite," he began, with the air of injured innocence he kept just for her. "You saw me!"

"I think he's shy," Ruby managed, faintly. "I mean . . ." She couldn't quite pin down exactly what she meant.

"Maybe he misses his kin." Thorne finally shut the door. "Been meaning to talk to you, anyway. You okay?"

No. "I guess." She trudged back to the table, settled in her chair. Thorne pulled out the guest chair, avoiding Gran's usual place even when she wasn't home. She stared down at the scattered paper. "Are you?"

"Not really." He watched as she picked up her pencil.

"Me either." She sounded small and defeated even to herself. "Thorne . . ."

"Want me to wait in the living room?"

It occurred to her that Conrad was probably jealous of *him*, too. And if she was honest with herself, he probably should be. She snuck a glance at Thorne's face, finding him gazing at the door to the hallway with an abstract expression.

What could she say? "I miss Hunter." If they talked about that, they wouldn't be talking about Conrad. Or anything else that was dangerous.

"So do I." He rested his hands on the table. Still not looking at her. "I . . . Ruby, if you found out something—like someone wasn't what you thought—what would you do?"

Uh-oh. She laid her pencil down again. So much for staying away from dangerous subjects. "What?"

"Like, if you found out something about this Grimtree—"

He can probably hear you. "Thorne, *please.* Gran expects me to at least try."

Kin

"I don't care what she expects." He'd gone pale. "I care about *you*."

It was the first time he'd said it so, well, openly. She stared, but he still wasn't looking at her. Thorne watched the doorway to the hall as if something was going to come through it, someone he heard but Ruby couldn't.

Something he feared.

"Would you take me instead of him?" His throat moved as he swallowed. His hands, loose and easy on the tabletop, didn't so much as twitch, but she found herself nervously keeping them in her peripheral vision.

As if he were Conrad.

"I'd fight him," Thorne said, very softly. "The old way, shift and claw. If you wanted. I know I'm not . . . I'm not Hunt, he could always make you laugh." A deep breath. "But I can try."

The sensation of being in a weird dreamworld where everything was reversed made all the breath leave her. Was this what being feytouched was like? There was little love lost between kin and the Children of Danu, but they'd been hunted together during the Age of Iron, and that sort of thing made them unwilling allies more often than not. Maybe she'd angered one somehow, and they'd hexed her for fun.

At least it wasn't the roaring in her ears. "Thorne . . ." A pale whisper.

"Just think about it. Who knows, I may challenge him anyway. Something's wrong, and I'm going to catch it." He shoved his chair back. He still wouldn't look at her. Ruby couldn't get in enough air to speak. What did you *do* when you couldn't breathe?

"Thorne . . ." She tried to find another word, *any* word, to slow him down. But he was already gone, without waiting for her to answer.

Maybe he was afraid of what she might say.

The front door closed softly, and she sat at the table, alternate waves of scalding and ice going through her. Her nose was full, and her eyes blurred with hot water.

Stop it. Look at your homework.

A drop spilled onto the worksheet, and she hurriedly brushed at her cheek as she heard footsteps on the stairs. Conrad, probably coming down to bug her again. Had he heard everything?

Maybe he had. If he did . . .

"You're still here," he said, from the door.

Ruby didn't look up. "I have to finish my homework."

Silence filled the kitchen, an invisible, dangerous fume like the bleedoff from a sylph-ether factory. She picked up her pencil, stared at the soft blue eraser at one end. The problems on the worksheet were spider squiggles. Moving as if charmed into sudden life, because she was blinking back more tears. Why?

If Thorne was serious . . . she would have to find some way

of stopping him. How? It wasn't like a Calc problem, a solution presenting itself as you followed all the steps. Once he got an idea in his head, it was *set*, and good luck changing anything.

Everything just kept going wrong. Hunter, a dead girl in the Park, Conrad . . .

You selfish bitch, Ruby. And she was. She couldn't hide from herself.

Because she'd felt *relieved* when Thorne said it. As if someone else could handle the problem, when it was her own damn thing to fix.

"He's a little too familiar with you," Conrad finally said, quietly.

Don't start. Please don't start. How could she balance the two of them? Conrad wasn't Hunter. She cleared her throat, swallowing more tears. "Mh." A noncommittal noise.

"I don't think you should talk to him."

"Fine." *You can't tell me what to do.*

She bent over the paper and tried to concentrate again. Conrad just stood there, but Ruby didn't stop until the garage door rattled, Gran coming home early. Which was Ruby's signal to flee upstairs past a silent, watching Grimtree boy, and splash some cold water on her aching, flaming face.

TWENTY-ONE

Saturdays on Southking Street were crowded affairs, but since Ruby hadn't been skipping to shop during the week, it was all she had. The press of everyone else who had a weekend day off to get their consumption on would have been all right, but it was still muggy and overcast, like breathing through a hot damp rag.

It wasn't made any easier by the fact that Conrad, while unwilling to be left at home alone, apparently hated shopping.

"You have everything." He looked good, at least—tanned and vital, white T-shirt, jeans on his long legs. "Why bother coming *here*?"

He kept scratching at the clan cuff on his left wrist as if it bugged him, but that was probably just nervousness. Some kin didn't like crowds. It was hard to contain the shift with mere-humans, even charmers, bumping soft and tantalizing against you with every step.

Ruby loved it.

"But I might find something *else*," she said for the tenth time, fingering a stack of thin silk blouses. The colors were all wrong, and the stall proprietor—mere-human, to be sure—had the lethargic, heavy-lidded look of a milqueweed smoker. The fabric was high quality, though, and she wondered if the man had paid import on it. There was an awful lot of silk coming in nowadays. Maybe she should ask Gran about that.

If she came home before Ruby went to bed tonight. The hunt for the killer wasn't turning anything up, despite the boy-kin cousins searching the Park for clues or scent. Whoever it was, they had covered their tracks thoroughly.

And Thorne hadn't been back to the cottage. She couldn't get him on the phone, either. Maybe he was avoiding her.

Conrad actually sniffed, disdainfully. "Like what? You have more clothes than you could ever get around to, schoolgirl." A faint note of disdain, and he bumped into her, a little harder than kinboys usually did. Ruby's hip hit the folding table the stall's wares were piled on, and the mere-human gave her a filthy look.

"Thanks." She slipped sideways, joining the flow of the crowd with practiced skill, and he grabbed at her arm, fingers sinking in. A jolt went up her arm, and she inhaled sharply.

"Let's go home." His fingers eased up, but she still felt the bruise rising. He grabbed at her hand next, thrusting his fingers between hers, and she wondered if Avery ever did this to Ellie. She'd never seen Nico and Cami holding hands, but they didn't have to, you could see as much shining in the air between them.

Conrad's hand was fever-warm, and hard. Did Cami or Ellie ever feel small or vulnerable next to their . . . boyfriends?

Was he her boyfriend? He wasn't a boytoy, that was for sure. He wasn't a cousin, either. Thorne would have been behind her, watchful and silent, his glower enough to keep a lot of trouble away. Hunter would have been to her right, clowning around a little like a Dead Harvest jester, pointing things out she might like, cracking jokes.

He could always make you smile. Her vision blurred, and her skin itched. The shift was there, lurking, even under inimical daylight. "I don't want to go home."

"Then give me the keys." He made a playful grab for her bag with his free hand, she turned away, almost stumbling into a jack with a leather jacket and weird, high, sharp cheekbones. Bone spurs, it looked like, and his cheeks were slicked with clear fluid, as if he was crying.

She looked hastily away, stepping closer to Conrad after all. *There's one big flaw in your plan.* "How will *I* get home, then?"

"Call and I'll come get you."

That makes no sense at all. "Fat chance." She tried to yank her hand away; maybe the movement surprised him, because his grasp tightened, small bones grinding together. *"Ow!"*

"Sorry." His lower lip pushed out a little. Was he actually *sulking*?

Kin

If any of the cousins sulked, you just left them alone. The boytoys didn't sulk, because as soon as they did, Ruby was gone, and no matter how many times they called, she didn't answer. She couldn't treat Conrad like that.

Right?

"Let go." She succeeded in pulling her hand away. Her nose was full, and all the thrill of shopping had drained away like water from a broken vase.

"Aw, don't cry, girlkin." He slid an arm around her shoulders; the heat of him tried to be comforting but just made her sweat more miserably.

Her bra was going to chafe, and her jeans were already uncomfortable. Plus, her hair felt like a wet draggle, and it felt like there was a rash beginning on her nape. She should have put the whole curling mass up, but she liked the way it looked spilling over her shoulders, against the thin crimson T-shirt.

Not now, though. Now it was hot as hell, and she could tell the curls were going to either go flat or become an unmanageable mass. *I love your hair*, Cami always said, her touch gentle as she combed or braided. *Mine just sits there.*

He guided her along, her head down and her gaze fixed on the pavement while she struggled to swallow the rock in her throat. Breaking down in a sobbing heap on Southking Street just wasn't done.

When she could look up, she found out he had steered her

onto Lowe Street and was making for the Semprena, parked down at the end. She usually parked on Highclere, but during the weekend everyone did, so you had to walk a little farther if you arrived after crack-of-dawn. Lowe Street was a little seedier, but still neatly kept, and the glossy black curves of her car sat comfortably among other heavy imported vehicles. You could tell the locals—those who didn't park in driveways had prime spots, their cars a little older but not old enough to be classic, a little dustier but not dirty enough to be deliberately masked.

Conrad stopped on the passenger side, and the heavy weight of his arm slid off her shoulders. Her cheeks were hot and her eyes still full, but she was able to tilt her head back and see him staring down at her with a curious expression.

Those golden irises were beautiful, but the tiny image of herself in his pupils was somehow . . . disturbing. She couldn't figure out why, because he leaned down, and his mouth met hers.

It wasn't like the shy peck on the cheek Hunter sometimes dared, or Thorne's trembling urgency. It wasn't like the hot need of the boytoys, either, like they were trying to get a mouthful of water in the desert.

It started out gentle, quickly turned demanding. He tasted of copper and heat and a weird acridity, of kin and wildness and musk. Before she knew it, he had backed her into the Semprena's side, and trapped between him and the car the urge to escape ignited inside her.

He caught her wrists, pressed her back, hot mouth and sharp teeth and the shift running inside her bones uneasily. His foot between both of hers, and she could feel that he was interested, very *definitely* interested in taking it further.

Just like any boytoy. But he wasn't. He was kin, and not cousin. Not safe. If she let him go too far, she'd end up married young instead of just betrothed, and that wasn't what she wanted.

Is it? I can't tell. It was too hard to think, between his mouth and his hands, cupping her face now that she'd stopped struggling.

He broke away and stared down at her. "Ruby," he breathed, that strange edge to his breath muddling her thinking even more. "I . . . God."

"Yeah," she managed, weakly. Funny, but the coldness all through her, independent of the muggy weather, had gone away.

"I love you," he whispered. Something lit in the back of his gaze for a moment, a small struggling spark. "I *need* you."

Maybe that was what she wanted to hear, because the tears brimmed over. He held her while she cried, again, helplessly, soaking his T-shirt. He stroked her hair, gently for once, and she couldn't help thinking about how much she wished he was someone else. At least she wasn't freezing inside, way down where nobody else could see.

TWENTY-TWO

TWO WEEKS LATER, RUBY LAY POKER-STIFF AGAIN, straight as a board. Stared up at the ceiling. Endlessly familiar white plaster, its whorls a map of her childhood country. This had been her room always, Gran said, and it was a toss-up whether the hazy memories of a white crib and sunshine were her own, or just from being told so many times about it.

Lots of other things were toss-ups, too.

Stop it. Just go to sleep.

Her bookshelf was organized by subject, author, title. All her clothes were folded, even the dirty ones in the laundry hamper by the door. All her mixtapes were packed in flat boxes under the bed, only the classical ones Gran kept buying her allowed to stay out, stacked alphabetically next to the stereo. Which never throbbed anymore; when she played it was softly, the sound tiptoeing around through the empty spaces where her comfortable mess used to live.

There was nothing left to organize unless she wanted to go

Kin

through her jewelry box. If she still couldn't sleep in an hour or so, she might do it, but then what would she do if she couldn't sleep tomorrow?

The entire cottage was breathless-quiet. No real rain yet, and everyone was getting tired of waiting for it. False summer was supposed to be cool at night, sunny during the day, not this sticky gray blanket and unmoving air. The trees stayed quarter- or half-turned, splashes of sickly color among the nasty, juicy green. The City Council had put out a circular, warning everyone to stay away from weather-charms. Even though they'd Twist you right down to the ground, someone might have been tempted. Sirens echoed all night in the distance, and there was a crime wave in the core—shootings, beatings, stabbings, theft.

People went crazy in this kind of heat.

Her arm hurt. If she looked, even in this dimness, she could probably see the fingermarks, deep sausages of bruising, sinking in and throbbing almost worse than when Conrad made them. Because she'd been on Babchat with Cami and Ellie to do her homework, for once, when he wanted to talk to her.

He was kin, but he didn't know his own strength.

Mithrus, just stop.

Deep breathing wasn't getting her anywhere.

She pushed the covers back, sat for a few minutes on the edge of the mattress. Staring at the window, where faint orange cityglow reflected from the oppressive clouds filtered past

169

the plane tree's branches. Leafshadows hung still and spiny, no breath of air to move them. The branch outside her window was still there.

It wasn't that being responsible was boring, really. There was a certain pleasure to be had in tidying up her room or even wrestling with her French homework.

No, the bad part was the sense of hanging from a cliff, her fingers slipping, and each time she got a good grip something else slipped.

Was that a sound, under the sirens? She was at the window before she realized it, tugging it up as cool-charmed air brushed her bare legs and arms. Easing it up, hoping it wouldn't betray her.

"What are you doing?" Her hip hit the sill and she winced, but her hand shot out and closed around a sweat-damp wrist. "Mithrus. Where have you *been*?"

"Thinking." Thorne caught his balance again, crouching on the branch. "Hoping you'd come out to play, so we could talk some more."

She tried to ignore the sharp pinch of guilt. Waiting for her, just like Hunter might have been? "I can't." *I'm trying to grow up, here.* "Why can't you be reasonable and come over during the day?" *And not leap out the door after telling me you're going to challenge Conrad and maybe start a diplomatic incident.*

"With *him* there, listening? Ruby, something's off about him. I can *smell* it. Look—"

"We're going to have an alliance." There. She'd said it out loud. "I have to."

He stared at her, the shadows dappling his face, turning it into another mask. His wrist turned to iron, but she didn't let go.

"You don't have to. There's things that . . . come out, Ruby. We'll talk. Please."

"I *can't*." What part of that did he not understand? Dampness, full of the smell of hot asphalt and rotting humidity, poured into her room. "Thorne—"

"You want me to fight for you?" He leaned forward a little, examining her expression. She hoped nothing showed. "Or does he make you happy? Just tell me he makes you happy and I won't say another word."

"Thorne . . ."

"Is it because I'm a boy-only? Or do you love him? Or is it Hunter?" Fierce whispers, the deep blue groaning scent of desperation coming off him in waves. "Mithrus Christ, just tell me."

How could she even begin to explain? "I *have to*, okay? Gran expects it."

"Then we'll go somewhere she can't find us."

Yeah. That will work. "Come on, Thorne. Please." It was like fullmoon, the silver thread dragging inside her. Only this was the wanting to slide out the window and explore the night with him, his fierce silence beside her familiar as her own breath. "Help me out here. Come by during the day, talk to Gran, and don't do anything stupid."

A pinprick of amber light flared deep in the back of his pupils, the shift running under his skin. Outside it a little too, fur poking up, blurring along his arm. "What's. That?" Thrumming under the words, felt more in the bones than heard with the ears. He was going to wake someone up. Gran, or Conrad.

It was anyone's guess which would be worse.

"What?" She glanced down, and realized she was just wearing a tank top and shorts to sleep in.

Thorne was staring at the fingermarks on her upper arm, dark and vicious. Maybe he could also see the hickey on the side of her neck, fresh and red-dark, but he wouldn't see the bruise on her hip or the one on her calf from Conrad accidentally kicking her, those big boots of his . . . and she *had* been walking slowly. He was accident-prone, maybe. Like some of the cousins—Marina, or gangly Peter Ardelle.

"It's nothing," she whispered, tugging on his wrist. "Okay, look, I'll come out, but only for a few minutes. I can't—"

"Who did that?"

"It's nothing. Look, Thorne—"

"Was it him?"

"Shhh, for Mithrus's sake keep it down. If they find out you're—"

"It was him." The pinpricks of light snuffed themselves, and she shuddered once, nervously. The smell coming off Thorne now was different. Darker, older, and even its familiar musk couldn't disguise the burning underneath.

Anger. More than anger.

She wet her lips, nervously, a flicker of her tongue. "Thorne. Please. Help me out here." *Calm down.*

He nodded, just like she'd said something profound. "Okay."

She nodded back, relieved, and her hand loosened on his wrist.

Maybe that's what he had been waiting for, because he tore free and dropped, landing silently below. A few leaves fluttered in the wake of his passing, and even when she leaned out, straining nose and ears, she sensed nothing. Was he already gone?

"Fuuuuuuuuuck," she breathed, a long aggravated sigh.

Another roiling of thunder under the stitchery of sirens, far in the distance over the Waste. She heard nothing else. Her arm ached, and the cooling-charms weren't doing nearly enough with the window all the way open.

She eased it shut, then stood with her eyes closed, listening. Nothing.

Back into bed, nestling atop the covers because of the heat. She was all set for another sleepless night, but the next thing she knew the alarm clock was buzzing like a minotaur's rage and it was time to put her cheerfulness on again to face another damn gray, breathless day.

PART III:

SHARP EYES

TWENTY-THREE

"GOING FOR A WALK," RUBY CALLED OVER HER shoulder, and hopped out the door. Gran was home, for once, but she was tired. If Ruby went fast enough, she could probably even make it past the corner and walk alone.

All the humidity made everything rundown as a pre-Reeve antique. The hollyhocks were going to seed, the other flowers just dying-back draggles. All the bushes gave the impression of drooping in the heat, and Gran's whitewashed picket fence looked sticky, like nasty frosting.

She made it out the garden gate, walking swiftly, head down, staring at her maryjanes against the pavement, little luckcharms jingling pleasantly. She hadn't even taken her school uniform off. Just one look at Gran's wan pale weariness had decided her. If Conrad followed her, Gran would *definitely* get some rest, but maybe he wouldn't, because—

"Good idea." Conrad fell into step beside her, and Ruby

had to suppress a twitch. He was so *quiet*. When he wanted to be. "Nice and private. Not like that place. Why doesn't she get a bigger house?"

She didn't sigh, though she was mightily tempted. He didn't like being treated like he was stupid. "She likes that one."

"Well, when it's ours we can expand it, maybe." He sounded pleased at the notion, and Ruby stole a sideways glance at him.

Today it was the blue T-shirt, which might've been good. He seemed a little more relaxed when he wore it. Of course, you could never tell what would upset him. He was . . . sensitive.

Maybe he'd been raised that way. It sounded like his brother had been the favored child. Grimtree clan seemed a nasty place to grow up, for sure. Sometimes Conrad mentioned little things they'd done to him, always reminding him he was lesser. It would be enough to make anyone a little touchy.

Besides, Ruby was one to talk. She had a reputation for temper, too.

"What do you think?" He smiled at her, easily keeping up with her hurried steps. "First thing I'd do is add on to that living room. Can't turn around in there without knocking something over."

"Yeah." *It's not Gran's fault you have those big long legs.* She didn't bother saying that she *liked* the living room the way it was, overstuffed furniture and reminders of Gran and clan and charming everywhere. She liked the tapestry, liked its shifting threads and slight comforting noises—except it had been silent a lot lately, the charmer's sun-and-moon looking abstract and worried.

Just like Gran.

"Then the bathrooms. Make the whole thing bigger. You know, you could just bulldoze the place. Start fresh." He reached for her hand, even though it was too hot to be touching anyone skin to skin.

She let him. If she was going to make the alliance work, she'd have to find some way around everything. Maybe this was growing up, you did what you had to do.

They reached the end of the block, and he tugged her to the left. "Come on."

"Where are you—"

"Where we can be alone."

"The only thing that way is . . ." *The Park*.

That was why Gran was so tired and worried.

The tabloids were still screaming. A housecleaner, merchuman, in the Market district, attacked at night. Cutting through the deserted streets on her way home from her job, right near the edge of Woodsdowne, almost eviscerated. If a patrol car hadn't happened around the corner as she stumbled out into the middle of the road, she might have died. As it was, she was in the hospital, and not really expected to make it.

Maybe whatever had killed Hunter was looking for other

prey. Or there were two killers, one strong enough to overpower a cousin and another . . . who knew?

It was enough to make you sick clear through. Gran had sat Ruby down at the kitchen table and issued another stern warning against any nighttime hijinks. *I know you are wont to go rambling, Ruby. Do not, at least until this is over.*

"We can find a nice little burrow in the Park." He was really looking happy. "We don't have to go back until dinnertime. Or later."

"Gran will worry—"

"Who cares? You're with *me* now."

"*I* care if she worries." *You should care too. She's Clanmother.*

"Awww. You're such a good little kingirl." It wasn't a compliment. His hand tightened, but only halfway. He didn't squeeze. "Who worries about *you*? You're just another piece to shove into the clan, to them."

Hearing someone else say it was uncomfortable, to say the least. Did it sound that selfish when she yelled it at Gran? On the other hand, hadn't Gran threatened to collar her? She let Conrad pull her along, and he gradually eased up on her hand.

"All those prying eyes," he continued, glancing around at the houses on either side of 23rd Avenue. "Makes you want to run."

After a full day at school and with the prospect of French homework to go home to, she didn't feel much like running anywhere, for once. Still, she agreed. "Yeah."

"Maybe we could go downtown once it gets dark. You ever been in the core?"

"No." *Are you insane?* She didn't ask. There was Tante Jeanette's house, with its white trim and cheerful red-painted door. Oncles Thorvald and John Elder had the one on the corner of 23rd and Tooth, with its picture-perfect garden. They were *étrange*, some said. It could have meant anything from "odd" to "in love with each other"; they held hands at the clan barbeques and were held to be the best teachers for young kin struggling with the shift.

"We could go. Just you and me."

"Are you kidding?" Sweat-soaked, her bra chafed and a trickle ran down her back. He was moving too fast, but if she tried to get him to slow down, he'd probably pinch her.

He flashed her one of those dangerous, white-tooth grins. "It's probably dangerous, but I'd be with you. And—"

"I'm not going into the core. Mithrus Christ, what's the matter with you?"

He dropped her hand, stopped dead. "What do you mean, what's the matter with me? I thought you wanted a little *fun*. I thought you wanted to run."

"Not into the core." She rubbed at her hand, though he hadn't hurt it. Maybe if he thought he had he'd be sorry, and—

"Oh. Too good to go with me, huh? Or are you afraid?"

"Neither. The core's just . . . I don't want to go."

"Come on. I dare you."

A while ago, she might even have done it. Now she took an uneasy half-step back. The honeysuckle along Oncle Val-jean's board fence exhaled an almost-clotted, spoiled sweetness. "What are you, five? I'm not going into the core. It's stupid."

The instant she said it, she regretted it.

Conrad's face had darkened. "Stupid?" he repeated, softly, and her skin chilled even under the assault of heavy gray-flannel sunshine. "You're calling *me* stupid? You can't even handle your French lessons without help from your little *friends*."

Ruby stared up at him. "I'm sorry, I—"

"Never mind." He spun away and took off down the sidewalk. Ruby followed, running to catch up.

"Conrad, *please*, I didn't say you were—"

"I thought you *wanted* me here! You asked me to stay!" He lengthened his stride, and fresh sweat beaded all over her. Her skirt swung, the luckcharms on her maryjanes still making that sweet music as she tried to keep up with him.

"I do want you to, I—".

"Like I don't know someone's been at your window, Ruby! Middle of the night, huh? The one who wants to fight me in shift? What if I tell your grandmother *that*?"

Oh, no. She skidded to a halt, the breath knocked out of her. "Conrad! *Conrad!*"

He broke into a run, the spooky-quick, darting speed of a kin on the edge of shift. The sunshine would hurt, would drive

Kin

pins into his eyes and rasp all over his skin, and it might madden him more.

"Please," Ruby said, softly, uselessly, watching him get smaller. He turned right on Tooth Street, heading for the Park. Or maybe even the core, though he'd have to cut across and go through the Market District before catching any of the main arteries leading in that direction.

She found out she was hugging herself, despite the awful, drenching heat. The cold inside her was back, and the two extremes fought over her so hard she trembled, the luckcharms jangling. Another thread of sweat traced down her calf from the hollow behind her knee, sliding over a fresh scrape.

If he told Gran Thorne was at her window . . . well, maybe it wouldn't be so bad.

Except he kept saying he'd go out in the Waste. That he'd rather die than go home.

That he loved her. She swallowed, hard, tears rising again. She used to be so tough, and now she was welling up all the time. She'd kept Cami and Ell from noticing so far, probably because both of them were so involved with their boyfriends. Did they ever feel like this? Was this what a serious boyfriend was like?

God, how did they stand it?

Maybe he just needed to run it off, and he'd come back to the cottage with it worked out. Maybe she could apologize enough, explain, and he would give her that frightening, intense, scary-delicious look, like she was the world and the Moon.

Like Thorne.

Her shoulders dropped. She turned, head down, and trudged back for home. If she stayed in the back garden, she wouldn't interrupt Gran's nap. It was almost too hot and wet to breathe, but Ruby deserved a little discomfort for what she'd done.

TWENTY-FOUR

THE CHARMBELL TINKLED SWEETLY, AND RUBY hopped off the couch, her French homework fluttering to the ground. "I'll get it!"

Heavy footsteps overhead—Conrad, probably coming to see what was going on. He hadn't come home until dinnertime yesterday, and he'd acted like nothing had happened. Which was a relief, but the breathless sense of waiting, trying to find a time to talk to him without Gran listening, was exhausting.

"Thank you!" Gran, home early from the office again today, called from the kitchen. A pot of spaghetti sauce was bubbling its scent through the entire cottage, a good strong red smell.

It's probably Thorne, coming to be reasonable. Her heart blew up like a relieved balloon, and she ripped the door open. Her cheerful *So there you are* died on her lips.

Tall even though he was slump-shouldered, a shabby older mere-human man stepped back hurriedly from the door. Wilted button-down and frayed tie, plaid sports jacket with shiny patches worn on the sleeves, and bloodshot, pale blue eyes that passed down Ruby in a brief flick before focusing over her shoulder. "I'm here to see de Varre." The words were as crisp as the rest of him was rumpled. What hair he had left was graying out of a dishwater brown, but there was a thread of rust in some of the ruthlessly buzzcut bits.

She smelled metal on him, and devouring sadness. The smoke-edge of determination. It wasn't until she noticed the holster under his left arm, a Stryker butt peeking out to say hello, that she realized he must be a cop.

Everything had gone still. What did he want? She hadn't done anything lately, not that she'd ever been guilty of more than a few curfew-breaks and fast driving, but—

"Detective Haelan." Gran, at Ruby's shoulder, didn't sound particularly welcoming. "A pleasure, as always."

"I don't like coming here any more than you like seeing me, Edalie."

Ruby's jaw dropped. Was he brave, or did he *know* her?

Gran's sigh could have won awards. "Will you come in, Christopher? I have Scotch."

He paled, and Ruby, her mouth opening slightly, watched his eyes narrow. Was he afraid? He was the one with the gun.

"This is business."

"No doubt." Gran's hand curled around Ruby's shoulder, and she squeezed, gently. Rube wouldn't have minded, except that was the shoulder Conrad had torqued when she got home from school, twisting her arm behind her back because she slammed the front door the way she always did.

He probably just meant to roughhouse a little, like boys did, but it still *hurt*. Right afterward he'd kissed her cheek and whispered, *I forgive you*. Which was okay, sure, but she wished she could just *talk* to him.

"Ruby," Gran continued, "please finish your homework upstairs. I'll call you for dinner."

"Okay." She didn't move, though, staring at the cop. Haelan. Where had she heard that name before? He looked familiar, but she couldn't quite pin it down.

Gran made a tut-tut noise. "Manners, child."

"Yeah." She slipped away down the hall.

The cop stepped over the threshold with a gust of hot, nasty-wet air. It smelled like old socks outside. "Cute girl. Looks just like—"

"She is *my* granddaughter." Gran sounded stiff. "Are you staying for dinner?"

He's not kin, why are you asking? Ruby took her time gathering up her scattered homework.

"No. Not staying." He took his battered shapeless hat off, exposing more graying dishwater-rust hair. "She looks like Katy."

"She should." Gran's tone had turned sharp. "Don't push me, *Detective*."

Even *more* fascinating. Now both of them were looking at

her, so she finished scooping up paper, pencils, notebook, index cards, and textbook. Ellie had suggested she use the cards, and so far, it was sort of working.

"Not trying to." He cleared his throat. The hat was shapeless because his hands worked at it while he held it, but not nervously. More like he wanted to squeeze something's throat. "Connie Teurung died this morning. Caparelli's breathing fire, but the Families are keeping the lid on him. We have a name."

Connie Teurung? It took a second for her to place *that* name. The woman who had been assaulted in the Market district.

She was . . . dead.

Oh, Mithrus. A thick lump of cold congealed in Ruby's stomach.

"And?" Gran, downright frosty.

"And we need your help."

"What more can I offer that I haven't already?"

"The . . . Edalie. Maybe you'd better sit down."

Ruby climbed the stairs, slowly, softly. Sometimes close quarters were useful. It wasn't until she got to the top that she saw Conrad, flattened against the hallway wall, sun-eyes a dull gleam.

They stared at each other. He edged along the wall, toward her, and he was so *silent.*

"I think I am *quite* ready to hear what you have to say." As calm as ever, but Ruby could imagine her shoulders going back a fraction and her eyes lightening, almost as pale as Ellie's now were.

Well, there's a name. Katy. Was that my mother?

"We got a tip. We searched a house, and we found the Kerr girl's backpack."

"That is very good news." Why didn't Gran sound relieved? The Kerr girl—that would have been the second body found in the Park.

The one that had parts . . . missing. Like Hunter's.

"The house was one of yours. We cordoned them. I'm sorry, but we couldn't take the chance that he would get away."

"Who?"

"One of the Arantzas. Danel. Hasn't been in school for a week, from what the parents tell me. They're spitting mad."

Ruby swayed. The roaring filled her head.

Danel. Except nobody ever called him that.

No. Mithrus, no.

Conrad's expression shifted, but she was too busy clutching the pile of homework to her chest.

"He had the girl's backpack?" How could Gran sound so *calm*?

"In his room, yes. Edalie, they can't find him." There was something odd about the way he said it—a little strained, as if he wanted to convey a different message.

"No." Softly. "Of course not."

Ruby folded over, trying to breathe. Conrad didn't move. Gran *had* to suspect she was listening. Hearing this.

It couldn't be. This was a nightmare, and soon she would wake up.

Danel. They *never* called him that, though. Ever since primary school, because of Hunter's teasing about his name, he'd just been called—

"It looks bad for him." The stupid cop kept talking. "Unless he's brought in, well . . . if there's another one, it's going to get worse. Already there's rumbles on the Council."

"I know. Thank you for alerting me to this."

"Edalie . . ." A cough, a creak as if he'd stepped on one of the living room's floorboards wrong. "Can I talk to her?"

"No."

"Edalie—"

Ruby bit her lower lip, savagely. The red-copper reek of blood squirted into her mouth, and she fought the shift, little tremors roiling under her skin.

They never called him that. He didn't like his first name, and he was spiky all the time. So Hunter called him *Thorne*, and it had stuck, partly because of his branchfamily's name. *Arantzas*, an old kin name, from the time before the Reeve.

And partly because it *expressed* him.

If you found out something about someone . . . No. Everything in her retreated from the thought. The cold was all through her,

Kin

no relief from the incessant sweating heat. Just another awful all-over sensation.

Gran's tone did not change at all. "No, Detective. You may leave."

He didn't get the hint. "I lost her too, you know."

"Leave. Now." Gran's iciest voice, and Ruby didn't wait to hear anything else. She scrambled silently for her door, and as she passed Conrad his lips skinned back from his teeth, white gleams in the dark.

Maybe he was startled by her sudden movement.

Or maybe he was smiling.

TWENTY-FIVE

Her nose and eyes were full of a thick green scent as soon as she opened the Semprena's door. The sky had darkened to the color of iron without the beaten-flat numbness that meant snow. Funny how the shades were so clearly distinguishable, yet if she had to, Ruby probably couldn't have explained it in words.

Ellie might have been able to, but she was at school with Cami. French class would just be starting, and here she was, skipping like the bad old Ruby.

Here on the Loop everyone was at work for the day. She left the Semprena tucked in the alley between the Paterson branch-head's house and the old biscuit-colored Basriat building. Not *everyone* who lived in Woodsdowne was kin; some of the mere-humans bought or rented because crime rates were low and the location was good. The Basriat apartments were in high demand, each one an exquisite little studio set around the jewel of the central courtyard. Oncle Zechariah ran it, and he was often to be found in the courtyard garden, coaxing something else into growing. He'd planned Gran's garden too, and trained the wisteria over the pergola in the tiny backyard.

This summer, the masses of purple flowers hadn't arrived. She'd been too frantic trying to find Ellie, then going to summer school, to wonder why.

As long as Oncle Zech didn't see her, it would be all right. She'd have yet another unexplained absence, but with Gran out of the house so much Ruby could just give some sort of story when Sister Amalia Peace-of-Ages called from Mother Hel's office.

Two blocks brought her to the Park. She popped a stick of choco beechgum into her mouth. Gran said it was a filthy habit, but some things just went better when you had something to sink your teeth into. Besides, if she was going to skip and be the old Ruby for the day, well, might as well go all the way, right?

I don't even know what I'm doing here.

It was like hunting, a persistent buzz in her bones. Except she didn't know what she was looking for. Her maryjanes slipped a little as she hopped the low stone wall, luckcharms making a subdued music.

Hunting and tracking both meant you had to have a clear idea of what you wanted. This itchy urgency, running along her skin like scratching wool, diffuse and exasperating, wasn't the same. This morning she'd accidentally closed her thumb in a drawer, set off Conrad by slamming the coffeepot down—her scalp still smarted a little from his sharp tug on her hair—almost run a few stopsigns *without* meaning to, and fidgeted all the way through History before deciding to just fuck it and get *out*.

Under the gray sky, Woodsdowne Park lay hushed and secretive. Here the green smell was so thick it almost made her dizzy, every plant exhaling in expectation. She stepped carefully, silent as Thorne, picking her way through dense undergrowth.

Maybe she wasn't *quite* the old Ruby. Because that girl would have simply gone in a straight line toward whatever was calling her. Now, though, she circled.

Ellie would be proud. She was of the opinion that you had to have a *plan*; any spontaneity drove her right up the wall. It made her fun to poke at, but now Ruby wondered if Gran would've been happier with Ell born into the kin.

Maybe. She sidestepped around a fallen log, its carpet of moss dried and crumbling, waiting for autumn rains to turn it green again. You'd think with the humidity it would have made a comeback.

It's not possible.

She winced. Playing dumb with Gran through dinner was sheer goddamn torture, but Conrad helped find other things to talk about. His acting skills were at least as good as Ruby's, because he was the picture of a tactful, engaging guest in a good mood. As soon as dinner was over Gran left, probably to start spreading the word that Thorne was to be brought to the Wolfmother—or to the police. Conrad? He'd gone straight upstairs and closed the guest room door.

Kin didn't do the things they were accusing him of. They just *didn't.*

And yet. Thorne and Hunter, jealous in the way only best friends—or brothers—could be. It was a clan joke that you never just said one, you always said *HunterandThorne*, all together in one breath, and looked for Ruby to see where they were.

He's not dom enough for you. Thorne, balancing outside her window. Holding the charmcooled cloth to her nape. No matter how fast or far she ran, sooner or later he'd show up, with Hunter along. The snarling they did over the boytoys, and Thorne's dark gaze sometimes, hot and scarily empty, when he regarded his rival cousin.

I didn't mean it! But she had. She *liked* the attention, liked knowing that she was wanted, not just tolerated because she'd accidentally been born rootfamily.

It couldn't be true. It just couldn't.

But there were three dead bodies and a girl's backpack saying otherwise. And Thorne's face. *What if you found out someone had done something?*

She'd stopped to fill the Semprena's tank and got a chocolate feymilk and a handful of tabloids while the wizened yellow-skinned jack attendant pumped the fuel in. The girl from Thrace Public—Annalise Kerr, gory grainy pictures splashed all over the thin cheap paper—was a redhead. Long, curling reddish hair.

Like Ruby.

That was one of the things about getting your news through the radio, you couldn't *see* things. The Teurung woman, the mere-human housecleaner? Her picture, too, showed auburn curls scraped back from her forehead.

Maybe it doesn't mean anything. Maybe they dyed their hair, lots of people do. Red's popular, it's good luck. It's a coincidence.

Yeah, right. The first girl victim just *happened* to be a girl who looked a little like her. Hacked at with something sharp, parts . . . missing. Connie Teurueng—the tabloids were full of details about how she'd been hacked at and . . . chewed.

Just like Hunter. What would hunt both kin and mere-humans?

Don't even think it. It can't be Thorne. It just can't.

And yet.

The pond was a still mirror. She edged along its rim, moving carefully through the almost-twilight. It was the middle of the day, but you wouldn't know it here. The heavy green smell meant rain, and the breathless hush was a little cooler than it had been. The little hairs on her arm and nape were tingling, as if a storm was on the way.

The rocks along the eastern edge of the pond were dry,

holding sun-warmth even now. She settled on her favorite one and braced her feet, wishing she wasn't in a skirt so she could pull her knees up and hug them. If she were younger, she wouldn't have cared.

Maybe that was the problem. The itching just wouldn't go away. There was something in the Park, but it wasn't here, where she and Hunt and Thorne had spent endless hours lazing around, talking about nothing, laughing, splashing in the shallows. Mudbombs thrown at each other, popcharms, and if she leapt up and ran just for the joy of moving she would hear them behind her.

The water was so still, reflecting branches and the dead-eye stare of the clouds overhead. An uneasy mutter in the distance could have been thunder out in the Waste.

She stared at the water while the urge to get up and find out what was bugging her crested and receded. Maybe if she just didn't go running off for once, she wouldn't make problems.

It was eerie, being alone. The cottage was small, but at least when she was worrying about someone else hearing her she wasn't thinking about how fucked-up she'd made everything. Or thinking about a body wrapped in linen, lowered into a grave, and the sound it made when he bumped against the bottom. The weight in her throat, and—

Her head jerked up. Ruby found herself crouching atop the rock, knees wide and palms flat, in defiance of ladylike manners. Her chin upflung, her hair a riot down her back, she tested the still air, inhaling in short little chuffs to get every scrap of scent.

What was that? A crunching noise? Something lost under more thunder, walking closer in great big steps across the sky? Like the feytale about Jath and the Giant, where as fast as Jath ran the Giant was only a step behind, swinging his axe.

No. Something else.

Ruby uncoiled, leaping from the rock and flashing through the undergrowth. No branch snapped underfoot, no leaf whispered at her passing—not until she heard it again.

A choked cry.

Someone's in trouble. Her speed doubled. Heedless, uncaring of her maryjanes, the luckcharms on the straps jangling discordant music now, she tore through brambles and crushed bracken. A weight in her throat was the silver-thin cry of *Help, the kin calls for aid*, but she denied it. If it was Thorne and she called a howl, things would probably get so bad she'd wish she had never—

Stinging pellets against her skin. The wind rose suddenly, thrashing in the treetops, as the poised storm trembled over New Haven. She burst into a small clearing, hail scattering and bouncing in tiny pinpricks, her gorge rising hot as the smell slapped her in the face.

The shape didn't make sense, especially with the branches heaving back and forth and the hail bouncing. Whiteness, spattered dark fluid like chocolate syrup, smooth knobs of knees flung wide, a tangled shock of hair.

Kin

A flash drenched the clearing. Pitiless white light, burning every detail into Ruby's brain. It was a girl, her hair dyed feyberry red, lying on her back as if asleep. Her face was tilted toward Ruby, slack and peaceful, her mouth a little open and her open eyes vacant.

Great gouges had been ripped out of the rest of her. She wore a public-school uniform, it was impossible to tell which one because the blazer was shredded, the skirt torn straight through. The dark fluid was blood, a brighter crimson than her dyed-red hair. Slashes—something had hacked cruelly at her middle, and her bare legs were striped with long claw-marks. She'd lost a shoe—not a maryjane but a scuffed brown loafer, and her foot slumped brokenly inside a filthy white sock.

The lightning-flash vanished. Ruby blinked, hot steaming sourness filling her mouth. She bent over, the remains of the apple she'd bolted between homeroom and History splashing onto a carpet of white hail. It even got into her *nose*, stinging and blocking that awful, brassy, nasty red smell she now knew was violent death.

No. Please no.

She could still *see* it, imprinted on the darkness when she blinked. A sound so massive it was almost silent rolled overhead, and the storm broke. The hail mixed with quarter-sized drops of smoking rain, a blurring silver curtain.

Ruby whirled, the maryjane strap on her left foot loosening dangerously, and ran.

She did not see the gleam behind her. Blind with panic, she pelted through the woods, and the low whistle of a blade cleaving air was drowned in the noise. Lightning crackled, and her pursuer flinched, spinning aside into the shadows, a low gleam of eyes near the ground as it crouched.

At the edge of the Park the strap snapped, and the chiming sounds of the silver bugle luckcharms scattering on pavement was lost as she flashed through the rain and stutter-bursts of lightning.

TWENTY-SIX

THE SEMPRENA CREPT INTO THE GARAGE THROUGH foaming rain, right next to Gran's crimson sedan. Ruby cut the engine and just sat there for a few seconds, shivering. Crystalline beads on the windshield, dewing the windows, but Gran's car was dry. She'd been home a while, then.

What am I going to tell her?

Later, every second she spent staring dully at the door to the utility room weighed on her. Each tick tock a separate little bead of guilt, a bracelet of *please, no, please, no.*

Finally, something occurred to her. She could see into the utility room, the corners of the washer and dryer stacked atop each other, the wooden slats of the flooring. The corkboard near the door to the kitchen, full of fluttering paper and the glimmers of spare keys, each neatly labeled.

Why would the door be wide open? The garage door too, she didn't even have to hit the opener.

The thought propelled her out of the car, wincing as her

left foot slid inside the broken-strapped maryjane. More luck-charms fell off, small bits of Potential popping as they hit the floor.

"Gran?" Someone else was using her voice again. Someone about five years old, and scared of the dark. *"Granmere?"*

The utility room door creaked a little as she passed. The chill wind pouring through would have been a relief if she hadn't felt so cold, her mouth sour and her nose still stinging.

She's not home. She went for a walk. Oh yeah, in this weather, sure. Maybe she was out in the garden, sitting under the pergola as she often used to, in an ancient, wooden, heavily repainted rocking chair. The squeak-thump of that rocker used to be the sound of long summer evenings, while Ruby chased fireflies with the cousins under Gran's benevolent gaze.

"Gran?" The kitchen light was on, warm yellow in the gray the day had become. Ruby's breath came high and harsh, the air had turned to glass. She couldn't drag enough breath in. Black flowers bloomed in her peripheral vision, soft and choking. "Are you home?"

The kitchen was just the same. Faded red linoleum squares, the cozy crimson countertops, the tomato-colored fridge under its layer of coolcharms humming away. A black enamel kettle on the stove, ticking as it cooled. A familiar smoke-edged breath— Lapsang Souchong, Gran's favorite tea. *Drinking fire makes you strong*, she said, but Ruby never . . .

A shattered porcelain cup, painted with delicate blue flowers. A curled hand, and a sob caught in Ruby's throat. She knew that hand, even though it looked so small and defenseless now. Unpolished nails, an old white scar, long healed, near the base of the thumb.

She took another step. The stool was knocked over, and a teapot stood sentinel on the narrow kitchen island dividing cooking space from eating space. Its spout was still steaming, and Ruby caught a whiff of something acrid under the smoke. She couldn't place it, because her nose filled up afresh, hot droplets sliding down her cheeks. Her hair dripped, too. She was wet clear through.

Her knees met the linoleum, her teeth clicking together painfully. "Gran? Gran, wake up . . . Gran . . ." Scrubbing at her nose with the back of her hand, everything blurring. It was a nightmare, again, and soon she'd wake up and Gran would be just fine, standing in the kitchen and frowning a little, abstracted, while Ruby ate breakfast and swung her legs, occasionally kicking her schoolbag. Back before everything got so horribly, awfully messed up.

A faint exhaling sound. Gran's hand twitched.

She's alive!

"Ruby." A low voice, male, familiar.

She craned her neck to look up. Everything inside her slammed painfully together, continents colliding. "Get the phone. Dial 733." *I sound like Ellie now.*

Conrad just stood there, staring down at her. Those sun-eyes looked vacant, the tiny image of herself on her knees next to her grandmother's curled-up body vanishing and reappearing as he blinked. He was soaked too, dripping onto the kitchen floor. Little rivers of rainwater, and his boots were caked with mud and moss. The clancuff at his wrist was dark with water, a line of red rash along its upper edge, rubbing at his forearm. His arms, bare because he only wore the blue T-shirt, steamed slightly.

Gran made another weak little movement, her hand clutching at empty air. Ruby grabbed it. *"Get the phone! Now!"*

He did, moving too slowly, as if in a terrible dream. Ruby threaded her fingers through her grandmother's, hoping she wouldn't bruise her. How could she look so *fragile*? What was going on? Some sort of attack? Kin didn't have heart attacks, or strokes . . . but kin didn't fall on each other and eat, either. *Or* on mere-humans.

"*Move it!*" she barked, the shift blurring inside her, and Conrad snapped forward as if compelled. It was dom-voice, Ruby's will flexing inside her brain and breath, forcing him to do as she said. "Dial 733. Tell them to hurry."

He picked up the phone, fumbled with the numbers, but in a few moments Ruby heard the crackle of a live connection.

"733, what are you reporting?"

"Something's wrong." Conrad licked his lips. "Uh, we're in Woodsdowne. One Woodsdowne Place. She's not moving. She's on the floor. I think she's dead."

Kin

Don't say that! Ruby ignored him, sliding her wet knees along the floor and slipping her arm under Gran's shoulders. The old woman seemed bird-light and too heavy all at once, her head lolling strangely. Ruby pulled her close, and maybe it was just the rain all over her, but Gran's skin seemed strangely . . . cold.

She threw her head back, the sound swelling inside her throat, and it burst out of her on a long trailing silver scarf. The howl bounced around the kitchen, spilling out through the utility door and the open front door—because Conrad, for some reason, hadn't closed it—and flashed through the rain outside. Everything in the cottage rattled together, and Conrad hunched his shoulders as the 733 operator cursed, a feedback squeal mottling the connection.

It ended, and Ruby sagged over Gran, savage exhaustion filling her to the brim. She inhaled to howl again, but faintly, through the rain, she heard an answering, double-edged cry.

Kin hear you, and are coming.

So she held the old woman close and kept repeating the only thing she could.

"Please, Gran. Please be okay. Help is coming. Please, please be okay . . ."

205

TWENTY-SEVEN

Trueheart Memorial was a soaring granite pile, one of the few buildings in the city that had survived the wrack and ruin of the Reeve. There were stories about people barricading themselves in there as the wild Potential roared over everything, changing and reshaping, the Great War drowning everything in fire and blood at the same time. Those who could found a hole to hide in, fighting off the Twists and the roaming packs of nightmare creatures, minotaurs and other, darker things boiling forth once the Age of Iron had ended.

Ruby hunched in a black plastic chair, hugging herself. They'd whisked Gran off and told her to wait, Oncle Efraim had disappeared with someone to do paperwork, Oncle Zechariah was on the phone at the nurse's station, making calls. Tante Sasha was at the cottage cleaning up; Conrad had stayed behind too. The cousins were all in school, and the adults busy, so Ruby was left to sit and shiver in a rundown waiting area with year-old magazines and two dying houseplants. Fluorescent light scoured her eyes, and she sometimes rocked back and forth, little nips and growls of pain all over her.

Shuffling footsteps, people hurrying. Low-voiced conversations. The whole place was alive with the smell of disinfectant and hopelessness. Her head ached, too. Her hair hung in her face, wet strings, and no matter how hard she tried to think of what to do next, nothing sounded even close to helpful.

The elevator at the end of the hall kept dinging. Each time, the sound hit Ruby on the skull like a hammer. It was annoying, to say the least, because she would just about get herself pulled together, ideas moving below the surface of her conscious mind—and then that little *ding* would go off and she'd lose it.

The light in here never changed, and she was hungry. But they'd told her to wait, so she waited, occasionally glancing down at the nurse's station. Oncle Zech disappeared between one look and the next, probably gone to find Oncle Efraim. Who else would be here? Tante Rachael, maybe, or Hunter's mother . . .

Ruby winced. She had to tell someone about the body. But who? Who would *listen*, and not immediately start making assumptions?

"Miss de Varre." He wasn't looming over her, but it was close. "Ruby, right?"

She looked up, and her heart lodged in the back of her mouth.

Detective Haelan smiled. It was a kind expression, but it

only made him look more tired. "I saw you the other day." Very gently, like he was afraid she was going to start screaming. "Can I sit down?"

She shrugged. *Knock yourself out.*

Same sport coat, same bloodshot eyes, same graying hair. Cheap harsh cigarettes and metabolized whiskey, a sharp, brooding scent somehow familiar, too. The chair next to her creaked as he settled into it, and he leaned forward, resting his elbows on his knees. It made her think of Conrad. For some reason that just made her stomach turn over a little more.

"You've had a hard day," he observed.

She was suddenly conscious that her hair had dried into a wild mess, her bruised and scabbed legs were striped with bramble-thorn scratches, and her muddy maryjanes had clearly seen better days, especially the left one. Her Juno blazer stank of wet wool, the shirt underneath it still damp with sweat and rain, and her toes felt raisin-wrinkled because her socks were wet. Her nose was red, because she'd been scrubbing at it, and her cheeks were probably chapped and inflamed.

I look like shit. A bitter little laugh jolted out of her, and she clapped her hand over her mouth to catch it. If she started now, she wouldn't stop until she was screaming, and nobody here needed *that*.

The cop didn't look at her, staring down toward the nurse's station. "They don't know what happened, but they think they have her stabilized." He swallowed, an audible click. His throat was probably dry as a bone. "They'll figure it out. She's strong."

You weren't there. She was so light, and . . . Ruby peeled her hand away from her mouth. Her voice cracked. "Who's Katy?"

Haelan closed his bloodshot eyes, briefly. Rubbed at the bridge of his nose with two fingertips, hard enough that the skin reddened when he took his hand away. "Mithrus. They don't even say her name around you?"

What could she say to that? It was impossible to explain the kin to outsiders. "Who is she? Is she still alive?"

"They never told you. Edalie never told you." He exhaled, hard, and she shifted nervously. "Katrina Rufina de Varre." Very quietly, and she got the idea he'd said it a lot. "You look a lot like her. The eyes, and your hair."

"My . . . mother. Right?"

"Yeah." He stared down at his scuffed brown wingtips. "She was . . . she was something."

I guess. "What did she do?"

"It's not what she did. It's what *they* did. To her." Another heavy exhale. "Look, this isn't . . . I shouldn't say anything. Edalie—your grandmother, she had reasons for everything. Some of them were even good ones. Sometimes I think they fought so much because Katy was just like her. Stubborn, both of them. Both thinking they knew everything."

Gran does know everything. That was a kid's thought, though.

What Gran didn't know about Ruby could fill a book, especially these days. "So she *is* dead. What happened to her? My moth—Katy." The name felt weird. But it was better than the word *mother*, because that one was empty. There was more comfort in *Gran*. Now there was a syllable to nail the world into place and make everything right again.

Except Ruby was suspecting nothing would ever be right again.

Haelan finally spoke again. "You really should ask Edalie."

"I don't think she'd tell me." *Nobody else will, either.* "I want to tell you something, though."

"What?" *Now* he looked at her, but Ruby kept staring straight ahead, pushing herself up out of the chair.

Maybe there was a cafeteria here, or something? Eating wasn't going to happen, but some limon would be nice. Tart, cold, and fizzing. It sounded like just the thing. "Thorne—you call him Danel. He didn't do it. He *couldn't* do it."

He was silent again. Just like an adult, not listening. There wasn't a damn thing Ruby could say. And if she told him about the body now . . .

A person. A redhaired schoolgirl. Someone was waiting for her to come home, probably worried because of the weather and the tabloids and . . . Ruby opened her mouth, closed it, hated the rock in her throat and the roaring in her head.

"Ruby!"

She looked up, dully, and blinked. It made no sense, and her immediate baffled response made no sense either. "You're supposed to be in school."

Cami, high hectic color in her cheeks, bent over and threw her arms around Ruby, squeezing with hysterical strength. Behind her, Ellie skidded to a stop, similarly flushed, her blazer askew and her wavy platinum hair ruffled. Both of them were gemmed with rain, and ambling in their wake was Nico Vultusino, looking years older than he should in a charcoal summerweight wool suit, his dark hair combed down for once.

He'd grown up. When had that happened?

The Family boy came to a stop and examined the cop next to Ruby, smiling that small, chilling little grin of his. "Haelan. Ministering to the victims again?"

"Vultusino." The cop didn't sound pleased. "I know the family."

"You know both Families. Funny how that works out." Nico stuffed his hands in his pockets. "What are we looking at here?"

"Waiting on toxicology screens. Woodsdowne's in an uproar. Caparelli's going to do something stupid before long."

"Must burn that he got promoted over you."

The detective tensed, but his words were crisp and even. "Well, the Canisari own him anyway, so no harm done, right?"

Nico's little smile intensified just a fraction. "Observe the proprieties, Detective. *La Vultusina* is here."

"Are you all r-right?" Cami barely loosened up enough for Ruby to breathe. "Nico got m-me out of class. Talked to Mother Hel, too."

Great. She couldn't say anything—Ellie had arrived, and put her arms around *both* of them. "Mithrus Christ," she whispered. "I'm so sorry, Rube."

Her mouth opened, but nothing came out. Instead, she curled into Cami's comforting warmth and shut her eyes.

"Nico." Cami stroked Ruby's tangled hair. "We're gonna t-take her home. Let Mrs. Fletcher know, okay?"

"Sure. Which car you taking?"

"Mine." The quiet note of pride almost hurt to hear. "Can you—"

"It's taken care of, Cami. Go on. If you go anywhere else, call the house if you need me, Stevens will know how to reach me."

"Okay. Ruby, we'll t-take you to the Hill—"

She finally got a word out. "No." Muffled against Cami's collarbone, which was weird because she had always been taller. "Home." She was shaking, and couldn't stop. If she spent the night with either of them she was going to start talking, and the last thing either of them needed were *her* problems vomited all over them.

They'd had enough to deal with. She had to deal with this, and she would.

Please let Gran be okay.

She took a deep breath, tried to stand up straight, and gently, very gently, worked her way free of their clinging, helpful arms.

"I want to go home," she repeated. "Please."

TWENTY-EIGHT

THE SPYDER WAS A NICE CHUNK OF AUTOMOBILE, cornered like it was on rails and purred like a kitten even though Cami didn't ask of it even a quarter of what it was capable of. The interior was butter-soft leather and smelled faintly of new car and lemon.

Cami drove agonizingly slow, obeying every traffic law to the letter. She even stopped *twice* at stop signs—once next to the sign, pulling forward to see what traffic was coming, and stopping again. It was like ripping out your nails, one at a time.

Still, it was kind of soothing to just lean against the door, put her fevered forehead against the glass, and listen to them try to make awkward conversation while the tires hummed. They tried to draw her out, but she didn't want to talk about it beyond *I came home and found her, that's all.*

They didn't ask why she skipped, or why she looked like she'd been rolled around in bushes and mud. The cop hadn't asked either.

When someone found the body—or when she told some-one—he would probably remember, though.

Katrina Rufina. She kept repeating the name, wishing the syllables could drown out the noise in her head. Why wouldn't the kin speak her name? Had she . . . maybe they didn't talk about her because she'd done something awful? Could that be it?

It's not what she did. It's what they did. To her.

"—Thorne," Cami said, and Ruby jolted out of the roaring.

"What?" She stared at the water on the window, fat beads rolling down. The lightning had backed off, but the rain showed no signs of slacking.

Cami punched the defroster. "I said, everyone's looking for Thorne. They're under strict orders not to hurt him, to bring him to Gran. Nico thinks—"

Words burst out of her. "He didn't do it. He couldn't have."

So much for staying quiet.

"Do what? All they're saying is that he's missing." Ellie, folded up in the backseat, leaned forward, her elbow resting on the side of Ruby's seat. "I've tried locator-charms, but no dice, and Livvie won't let me do anything real high strength. The charm-stitcher keeps scaring her."

Because your stepmother almost broke your charming. Or that thing you were staying with almost did. Ruby suppressed a shiver. "Everyone's looking for him."

"I thought *you'd* know where he was." Cami stared past the wipers, their steady rhythm a heartbeat. Her slight frown of concentration just made her more beautiful.

Ruby's entire body itched. "Well, I don't." *If I did, I wouldn't tell anyone. Not until I could talk to him.*

Ellie made a clicking noise with her tongue. She smelled like expensive fabric softener, a faint edge of active charming like cherries, and the good green of approaching rain. "We were kind of relieved you'd skipped, until we both got called out of class. Did you know Nico even tried to walk into Juno's? Mother Hel had to come out on the steps and talk to him."

"I don't think I've ever seen him so polite." Cami's shy laugh, soft and musical, shriveled everything up inside of Ruby.

How could she *laugh*, with everything going on? Ruby sank her teeth into her lower lip, just on the edge of drawing blood. Again.

It sort of helped.

Not really.

Ellie made the peculiar little chuffing noise, not quite a laugh, that meant she was amused. "Well, at least he's got *some* sense."

"Not as much as I'd hoped. But it's developing." Cami turned right, then left, then right again, and they were three blocks from the cottage. "Ruby . . . are you s-sure you want to go home? I mean, it's probably better if you're . . . with us. You know?"

"I need to be home." Her lip stung as she forced herself to say it quietly. "We've got a guest. And if—*when* Gran comes home, it has to be clean."

The Spyder crept along, its wheels pushing water aside. The windshield wipers kept doing their job, like the idiots they were.

"Conrad," Ellie said finally, and Ruby almost gave a guilty start. "So . . . maybe we can come in and meet him?"

Oh yeah, that'll go over really well. "Now's not a good time."

"Well, when is?" Ellie persisted.

"Ell . . ." Cami sighed.

Ruby gathered herself. "When it is I'll let you know. Let me out here, Cami."

She kept the Spyder to a creep. "It's still r-raining."

"I could get out and walk faster than this."

"Don't." Ellie's fingers on her shoulder, rubbing a little. "We want to help, Ruby."

There's nothing you can do. "You've got your own problems." She played with the door-catch, scraping her broken nails over the silver bar. She wasn't even wearing any polish.

"You *are* our problem." Ellie squeezed a little.

Ruby almost flinched. *Maybe that's what Conrad thinks too. That I'm his problem.* "I'm nobody's problem." *Besides, I'm a self-ish bitch, remember?* She stared out the window, willing the cottage to appear. Everything was blurring, running together.

Or maybe it was just that her eyes were leaking.

"That's not true." Cami pulled to a stop. "We're your *friends*, Ruby."

Funny, how she remembered being in the driver's seat, and trying to convince Ellie of the same thing. *Stop being a selfish bitch. I realize it's your default, but just try.* "There's nothing you can do right now. Thanks for the ride."

She was out of her seatbelt in a hot second, and out in the rain before Cami could say anything else.

The flagstones were a little slippery, and the front door was still open. As if Gran wanted fresh rain-washed air, or she was expecting someone.

But Gran was in a hospital bed. She was old, and it wasn't like kin to just *collapse*.

Maybe she didn't just collapse. You ever think of that?

Of course she had. She'd been spending the entire time sitting there trying *not* to think about it.

Maybe once she got inside, she could just close the door and go upstairs. Lie down. Rest. Figure out how to fix the gigantic mess that had just descended on the world.

She trudged through the rain, her left maryjane flopping a little and her eyes still welling with hot water. She didn't see the gleam in the upstairs window, a pair of eyes watching her from the guest room. Golden eyes, narrowed and thoughtful.

And frightfully, scarily empty.

PART IV:

WHAT SHARP TEETH

TWENTY-NINE

EVERY WINDOW AND DOOR ON THE FIRST FLOOR WAS open. She wrestled them closed, her arms aching savagely as if she'd been playing hang-me-man all day in the Park with the cousins. With that done, she made her way upstairs, step by painful step. The dishes were washed and the floor freshly mopped; Tante Sasha had probably run home to make dinner for her family. She had three boys, and they were all growing. The silence said she'd taken Conrad with her, though she hadn't left a note.

Ruby wanted a shower, but just getting into dry clothes was all she had time for. Because after that she would clean the house from top to bottom, so that *when* Gran came home, she could see that Ruby had been responsible and grown up, a good kingirl.

Jeans, tank top, a cerise silk jumper—the one she'd met Conrad at the train station in, it felt like a lifetime ago. Her uniform was filthy, her socks worse, and nothing was going to save that left maryjane. There was one tiny luckcharm still clinging to the strap; she stuffed it in her pocket and started dragging a comb through her tangled, air-dried hair. Her schoolbag lay on her bed, a rain-darkened blot, and it would probably leave a mark on the comforter.

Her head had turned into cotton fuzz. It was a welcome change from the roaring.

Dry socks felt good. Her old battered trainers were just right. She gathered up her uniform, holding it crumpled in a ball at arm's length as she smelled the sweat and fear and desperation on it.

Underneath, the faint brassy note of that awful, awful sight.

She turned, meaning to head out the door and down to the utility room—the whole uniform, blazer included, needed a good soaking—and dropped the entire ball, letting out a choked cry.

Conrad leaned against her doorframe, his eyes reflecting gold from the overhead light. For a moment they were too big and luminous, and a ripple ran through him as if he was going to shift, the points of his ears lengthening . . . and receding.

Ruby's heart threatened to explode. "Mithrus *Christ*!" she hissed, forgetting how much he didn't like being told what to do. "Make a little noise next time! You *scared* me!"

"Sorry." He didn't look sorry. Instead, he looked thoughtful. "Where are you going?"

"Downstairs, to put this in the . . . have you been here the whole time? Did Tante Sasha go home?"

"So many questions. You always ask a lot of them." He nodded, as if he'd said something profound. "I think it's time we talked."

I don't have time for this. "I've got to get the house cleaned up. Plus I have to make dinner. When Gran comes home—"

"Is she coming home, then?" Why didn't he sound interested?

"Of course she is." Ruby bent to pick up the stinking uniform. "I mean, she's stabilized. That's what the cop said."

"Cop?"

"Yeah. Haelan. The one who came . . . came by and said . . ." She straightened, slowly. "Why were all the windows open? And where were you? Did you just come home when Gran—"

"Ruby, shut the fuck up." Calmly, quietly. "Or I will beat the shit out of you."

Her jaw dropped. She stared at him.

He held up his hand, slowly, and something fluid silver dangled from it. Alive with its own light, it twisted and turned, curling around his fingers. Its scales rasped against his skin, and Ruby's entire body chilled.

It was a collar. Those scales would draw tight around the throat, and the *shift* would be inaccessible. Your senses would dull, only mere-human instead of the sharpness of kin. No more fullmoons either, unless the keyholder decided you could control yourself.

If he was holding the collar, he had the key, too.

"This is for your own good." Almost kindly. He stopped leaning against the doorframe, drawing himself up, and the small satisfied smile he wore made his face into a stranger's. His teeth were very white. Kin-white. "Your grandmother would agree."

She took a single step back. *What do you know about what Gran agrees about? You're Grimtree, you're a guest.*

"Don't make this hard." He moved forward, and his smile widened. His boots crushed her uniform, and in a blinding flash, Ruby saw the mud—dried now—coating them.

The same as the mud on her maryjanes.

"You were in the Park," she whispered. "You were . . . you . . ."

A zing, like biting on charmed tinfoil, all the way down her spine. Her brain refused to put the pieces together, but her body knew.

A snarl drifted over his face, a cloud over the sun. "You go poking in where you don't belong. It's going to take some training, but you'll learn."

Training? "What are you *talking* about? Look, put that thing away. You can help me make dinner, and we'll just—"

"*Don't tell me what to do!*" he screamed, and lurched forward.

THIRTY

AFTERWARD SHE WASN'T QUITE SURE WHAT HAD HAPpened. She only remembered bits and pieces. First the red flare of agony when he backhanded her, kin strength making the blow just short of neck-snapping force, and a welter of confusion with her desperate screams and his growling roar. The bed—she'd fallen, half-sideways, and was scrabbling, the comforter tearing and her fist tangling in the strap of her schoolbag.

He grabbed her hair as she slid off the bed on the other side, her scalp searing red-hot as she tore free, and somehow she was on her back, her knees drawn up, and she *kicked*, catching him square in the jaw. He went over backward, the collar making a jangling sound as it was flung in an oddly perfect arc, smacking against her bookshelf and spilling downward.

Somehow on her feet, lunging for the door, trainers slipping in the pile of damp uniform, and she was in the hall, hearing his cheated howl behind her.

He's going to be so angry.

A noise—breaking glass. Had he broken the window? Her mirror? Bad luck, just like in a feytale.

He was in the Park, a cold, rational, almost-adult voice in her head spoke up, quietly and calmly. *Get out of here, Ruby, before he kills you too.*

She blundered down the stairs, trapped in the syrup of a bad dream. The nightmare just kept getting worse, and worse, and she was beginning to suspect there was no waking up.

She'd locked the front door, and now her fingers plucked at it, clumsy with terror. Heavy footsteps on the stairs behind her, and that awful, rasping, jangling sound.

"Quit running. I *love* you. You're my way out, Ruby." His nose sounded clogged—had she broken it? Oh, God, he was going to be so *angry*, and after weeks of seeing what he could do when he was just *irritated* she just didn't even, oh *God*, her fingers would not work on the deadbolt, just scrabbled blindly. "We'll just get this on, and then you'll be mine. All mine."

Mithrus please oh please—the lock suddenly yielded, she ripped the door open and almost tripped over the threshold.

"*Ruuuuuuby!*" he roared behind her. "*YOU'RE MIIIIIII-INE!*"

The roaring was all through her, a red madness, and sky-tears spattered her face and hands as Ruby fled into the gathering, rainy dusk.

THIRTY-ONE

WHERE DID YOU GO, WHEN THE WORLD HAD BECOME
a carnival-mirror reflection? All distorted, nothing in its right
shape.

She ran for a long time, splashing through puddles, dodg-
ing headlights and the screaming of horns, the screech of tires.
Dashing across streets, keeping to shadows like any hunted animal, as the sky gathered indigo folds close and began to dump
water on New Haven in earnest.

As soon as full night fell, the shift bloomed inside her bones;
the confusing patchwork jumble of streets, pouring water and
bright headlamps, black-wet trees shaking off scab-leaves and
showers of droplets was a Dead Harvest nightmare.

Every time the wine-fume of terror inside her retreated a
little, she heard footsteps behind her. The scream was still echoing inside her head, weirdly modulated as if falling into a well.

You're miiiiiiine!

After a long while the rain slacked, she smelled trees and water and crushed green, and the thought that she was perhaps in the Park brought her to a shuddering, sweat-soaked halt.

Blinking, stumbling, she fetched up against a huge oak tree, every bruise and scrape suddenly demanding to be heard, a chorus of pain. The shift retreated all at once, water through a sluice, and her sides heaved with deep gasping breaths. It was too dark, her eyesight no longer as sharply adapted for a long moment as she altered into baseform. The ripples under her skin retreated, she coughed and blinked more, rainwater and salt-sweat stinging her eyes.

Where am I?

It wasn't Woodsdowne. Hot, massive relief filled her, and she glanced nervously around, straining her ears. No footsteps. No cars. It was quiet.

What . . . oh. I know.

Another jolt of relief, so hard and fast it thumped her in the stomach a good one. She bent over, struggling with nausea, long strings of her wet hair falling in her face.

It was the park atop Haven Hill. She could see glimmers of city light through the trees, and the edge of a parking lot. Wet streetlamp glow ran on the paved surface, and she could see enough of the shape to know it was the south end. It probably would have been developed before now, except all around it were the estates of the rich—mostly Family, they liked to settle up high. The charmers lived around Perrault, and Woodsdowne was its own little country.

New Haven was a collection of parts, and all of them were jumbled now.

She swayed, her nails driving into tough bark. The wind had gentled, a steady north keener, shaking fat droplets out of the treetops. The heat was gone, swept away just as a broom would slide across a kitchen floor.

Kitchen. Red linoleum squares, and Gran's hand, so small and still. Conrad, just standing there, dripping . . .

Don't think about that. Her brain shut down. Shivers gripped her, great waves of them, her teeth chattering and her hair swinging, tapping her cheeks.

Something else swung too, bumping her hip. Ruby looked down.

It was her schoolbag. She'd grabbed it as she went over the bed, probably, and habit had made her keep hold of it.

The thought of herself half-shifted and running all the way through New Haven carrying her French textbook suddenly struck her sideways, and she bent over again, this time wheezing with laughter.

It hurt, and there was a screamy, breathy quality to it she didn't like, but it wasn't sobbing. So there was that.

A couple times she thought she was over it, but then the image would pop up again, just like a Fish Day paper puppet,

LILI ST. CROW

and she would be off on another jagging run of hilarity. Still, it couldn't last forever, and when the paroxysm retreated, she found herself striped with mud and drenched—*again*—cold, and having to pee something fierce.

It was then she found out that no matter how badly she'd wanted to sneak out and prowl at night, all it took was not being able to go home for her to wish she was there, warm and safe with Gran sleeping in her bedroom and the rain beating on her window. The plane tree's shadow would make familiar shapes on the sill, and she would fall asleep to recognizable, comforting sounds.

Can't go there. He's there.

Well, where else was there to go? Cami and Ellie didn't need this. Conrad was *kin*, and he was likely to be unstoppable if someone got between him and Ruby. Nico might have a chance at taking him on . . . but her brain just gave up thinking about *that*, too.

She wasn't smart like Ellie or kind like Cami. She wasn't strong like Gran. All she was . . .

Selfish bitch. You probably made him awful, just like you made Thorne and Hunter turn on each other. You probably made Gran collapse, too.

Any way you looked at it, she was poison. Trying to change into what Gran wanted at this late date was an abject failure. Now there were people *dead* because of her.

That was another thing. The body in the Park. Who could she tell *now*?

That detective. Haelan.

Would he even believe her? He'd decided Thorne was guilty; would she just be making it worse? Either way a girl was *dead*, lying there in the rain, and Ruby was the only one who knew.

Not the only one. Who killed her, Ruby?

She didn't want to think about that.

You have to. Whoever killed her probably killed Hunter and that other girl. Put her backpack in Thorne's room. Who would do something like that?

Who would believe Ruby if she told? She was held to be Wild, and flighty, but not an outright liar. Still, she'd have to choose who to approach. If she could somehow manage to pour out her imaginings, if they would sit still and listen long enough . . .

A purring broke the silence. She straightened, glancing around wildly, and the shift boiled underneath her skin again: *fight or flight, fight or flight?*

The sound drew closer. A sword of blue-white sliced the darkness, stinging her night-adapted eyes. The wind rose, a fresh shower of cold water spattering across her.

It was a car. Who would be up here? Teenagers looking for a makeout spot?

It's Wednesday. Nobody is going to come out here to snog at this hour, not with school tomorrow.

She couldn't make out the color of the car, but she was suddenly, deadly certain it was a black Semprena, its engine making a familiar sweet sound and a pair of grasping, pinching, pulling hands at the wheel, one of them wrapped with a fluid silver chain.

Even if it wasn't, this was not a place to be found after dark. Ruby showed her teeth, catlike, and fled.

THIRTY-TWO

THE REST OF THAT ACHING–COLD NIGHT PASSED IN a blur. There was the unfamiliar façade of Southking Street at night, hard-faced jacks and different tents than the regular daytime booths. Poisonseller, blackblade knifemartin, sellers of curse and hex, the gangs on every corner shooting warning glares and raucous laughter into the street when someone passed. The only areas brightly lit were the food trucks, most of them with a beefy jack or two running the night shift and deterring trouble just by their size alone.

Ruby faded back into the shadows and cut over to Highclere, where she usually parked. Nothing for her there either; sleeping in someone else's backyard wasn't a good idea. She circled for a while, aimlessly, until a foggy idea crawled up out of the adrenaline-drained mush inside her skull.

Now that she had a destination, she was aware of just how tired she was. It was a long way away, and no car to take her there. She also had to stay alert, sliding through shadows, her heart rabbiting inside her ribs every time she saw headlights or heard a noise.

Hours later—she wasn't sure how many, just that it was still dark and even the sound of traffic had faded to a faraway mumble—she turned a corner and saw the long shot of Kelleston Avenue, shuttered and sleepy even though the streetlights still buzzed and cast circles of glow around their feet.

I drove here. With Cami and Ell. There had been a low hulking shape chasing them—a minotaur, a monster of rage and pain birthed from the core's stagnant sickness.

She'd always thought that's where the monsters came from—*somewhere else.* Not her own house.

Ruby shuddered. But if she was on Kelleston, it meant her goal was in range. There was something else, too.

Halfway down the street was a callbox, the shiny phone sitting under a glare of buzzing fluorescents. It was a half-shell instead of an enclosed box, and that light meant anyone could see her a mile away, but she didn't care. She walked, a little unsteadily, her trainers slightly squishy. Her hair was a wild rat's nest, and she supposed she looked like a wandering jobber. If a police patrol saw her, maybe they'd take her in for vagrancy. At least until they found out she was under eighteen and dragged her downtown for breaking curfew.

Then they'd take her back to the cottage, and that was where she absolutely, positively couldn't go.

She stopped, her head tilted, decided she hadn't heard anything. The callbox glowed, and when she finally reached it, leaning against the scarred glass side of the cubicle, a wave of weariness so intense swamped her she seriously considered sinking down on the pavement and sleeping right there. The hazy idea that the light would keep her safe was so compelling she actually closed her eyes for a few moments.

A contrary, nagging impulse wouldn't go away. So she picked up the receiver. A dial tone greeted her, and the charming on the box sparked a little as she dug in her schoolbag. A single quart-pence, round and silver, slid into the phone's innards, and she dialed.

Crackle. Buzz. *"733, what are you reporting?"*

It took two tries to make her voice work. "I have a message, for Detective Haelan."

"This isn't an answering service—"

"I *know*." Wouldn't *anyone* let her talk? "There's another body in Woodsdowne Park. A girl. Public school. She . . . she has red hair." *Like me. Mithrus, did I . . . was it that I . . . ?*

A short silence. She could almost *feel* the woman willing her to say more. There was a ghost of other voices on the line, whirring and buzzing.

"Okay. What's your name?"

"He didn't do it. Danel didn't do it. Tell Haelan that. I know who *did*, but you can't catch him. He's dangerous . . . and . . . and . . ." What was she trying to say? She lost the thread, staring down Kelleston. Why was her heart suddenly thundering? And her eyes watering.

"Miss, are you still there? Miss? Tell me more. Where are you? Who is this?"

Headlights. Creeping along, and the car eased out into a pool of streetlamp shine.

It was black, and glossy, and low-slung.

Ruby slammed the phone down and spun, her quart-pence discharged from its innards with a chiming click—of course, you didn't need to pay to dial emergency, why was she suddenly so stupid—and ran for an alley that would cut through to Cleverjack Street. Behind her, the engine gunned, but she made it just in time and kept running. There was a screech of tires, a crashing noise, and she sprinted for all she was worth, bursting out onto Cleverjack with her schoolbag bumping her hip and her eyes white-ringed with terror. Houses flashed by, the occasional small café or storefront dead and dark just like Kelleston's buttoned-up buildings, and if she could just get to 79th she could cut up and be in familiar territory, under whispering black-barked elms.

Head down, fists pumping, the shift burning as she used every ounce of speed and agility it could give her tired body, Ruby ran for the last place anyone would expect her to go.

THIRTY-THREE

St. Juno's was downright eerie at night. For one thing, it was dead quiet, and the bulk of the nunnery on the other side of the lacrosse field, where the Sisters went when they weren't at the school, looked weirdly insubstantial. Maybe because the field itself was full of ground fog, rising in thick white billows that made her shiver. She'd often wondered whether you could catch the Sisters coming across the field if you got to school early enough, their black robes swinging and their head coverings magpie-colored in the predawn hush.

She hunched her shoulders, digging in her schoolbag. There was a folded square of charmed tinfoil in one of the pockets—it was one of those things every self-respecting girl up to no good needed at all times. Tinfoil held minor charms like a dream, and it broke some lockcharms and certain alarm-chain charms without alerting anyone. A girl with any sort of charm ability and the patience to keep trying until she got it right could learn how to slip a square of folded tinfoil through a tiny aperture and work on the lockcharm from the *inside*, suppressing the alarm-chains with a sort of relaxed, focused attention. Ruby always kept a couple spares in her bag, folding and charging them when Gran wasn't home, and she'd kept Ellie and Cami supplied with them all during middle school. Not that either of them used them when Ruby wasn't around.

You could never tell when you'd need to stage a break from education, and since neither Ellie nor Cami was brave enough to go on their own, it was up to her to drag them into having a good time *and* ensure they could leave school grounds.

Only this time, she was trying to get *in*.

Getting on school grounds had necessitated climbing a weirdly corkscrewed oak at the north end of the high stone wall closing Juno's off from the rest of New Haven. Dropping down on the other side had rattled her teeth, and she supposed she should just be grateful the charm-laid defenses didn't decide she was a danger at this hour.

The rain had stopped. High scudding clouds filled the sky, and it was *cold*. Her fingers were numb, but her teeth had stopped chattering. She supposed she should be vaguely worried about that, but it didn't seem important.

What *was* important was this door, leading out from the main gym onto the lacrosse field. It had been loose the last time they'd had to go out for Phys Ed, sweating under the hot gray blanket-sky. Cami's surprisingly hard toss of a dodgeball. *Go get 'em, Cami!* Ellie had yelled, a bright piercing happy noise over the chaos of other girls shrieking and slipping in wet grass.

It was, thank Mithrus, still loose. She slipped the charmed tinfoil through gently, delicately, her other hand on the lever. The door buzzed, Potential uneasy, its net of charm and defense only half-mollified by the fact that she *was* a student, and hence, familiar.

"Please," she whispered through numb lips. "There's no prohibition against me coming *in*, just leaving before lastbell. *Please.*"

The tinfoil sparked, there was a slight stinging in her fingers, and the door opened with a slight begrudging groan. She nipped through, smart as you please, and was plunged into darkness when it closed behind her.

A small sobbing sound finally escaped her. The gym echoed, enough faint glow filtering in through the high wire-shielded windows above the bleachers to let her see once she took a breath and really looked around.

The wooden floor was just the same, its painted lines for ditchball and basquetoz glowing faintly with anti-cheating charms.

Ruby sagged against the door. The defenses humming against her back, meant to keep all sorts of things away from vulnerable young Potential-carrying girls, were comforting but scratchy, like a wool blanket. Her nose filled with the tang of old sweat and greased wood, chalk and the familiar, indefinable odor of *school*.

There was at least a dry pair of panties in her gym locker, maybe a shirt that didn't reek too badly, and probably a snack too. She could find somewhere in this great big stone pile to sleep, and in the morning she could figure out what to do next.

At least she'd told someone about the body in the Park. She shivered, and the temptation to just slide right down and pass out on the floor was amazingly strong. It was weird how just doing something simple, like calling Emergency and blurting out a secret, could make a huge weight shift from your shoulders.

There was plenty else pressing down on her, though. Ruby forced herself to move away from the door. Her footsteps squished, trainers squeaking. Was she leaving footprints?

I'll worry about that later, she told herself, and headed for the locker room.

The school had been a Mithraic cathedral once, and there were all sorts of interesting, forgotten places curled up in its warren of passages. The choir loft, for example, behind a carved-stone frieze that was delicate enough to be charm-worked, but was a relic from the Age of Iron. There were a couple places in the library nobody ever went unless they were hiding, and there

Kin

was a small rundown shed in a copse on the side of the lacrosse field—the side that wasn't the gravel driveway, the ancient barn that was now storage, *or* the nunnery and its attendant gardens.

None of those places were what Ruby wanted. She ghosted through the refectory, long narrow tables charmwaxed and gleaming, took a hard right through the double doors, passed banks of lockers and what the students called Death Alley—Sister Eunice Mithrus's Blessing's Science classroom on the right, Sister Margaret's Ethics and Deportment on the left. Somehow, Sister Margaret always *knew* when you were trying to sneak down this hall, and Ruby held her breath and crossed her fingers as she slid past the frowning black oak door. Ethics and Deportment was Year Nine, but Mithrus Himself couldn't help you if Sister Margaret saw you in the refectory with your knees crossed, or caught you bending over to pick something up in the hall instead of sinking down with your knees together and scooping it up without your skirt riding up to show what she called Your Treasures. Whether she meant *your panties* or *what's underneath yon panties*, Ruby never figured out.

She'd managed a frigid locker-room shower and was marginally cleaner, and at least the mud and branches were out of her hair. Down past more lockers, tucked behind an ancient age-blackened stairwell that led up to the Drama loft, where the club of wannabe actresses spent all their time (and smuggled in honeywine coolers whenever they could), yet further down.

She ran her fingertips along the metal lockers, wincing a little as broken fingernails scraped on layers of chipped paint.

One break in the lockers for a restroom, another break for a broom closet . . . and the third, she felt for the knob and breathed a little prayer.

It was open.

Another half sigh, half sob of relief, and Ruby slipped through. There were stairs going down, and it was perceptibly warmer. The ancient boiler was down this way, and these back hallways were crammed with useless junk and welcome warmth. Her fingers and nose tingled, and her teeth were chattering again. Which was odd, because it had *finally* warmed up.

There were all sorts of nooks and crannies down here, and nobody would find her.

Hot water splashed on her collarbones. She was leaking again. She passed a stack of old hymnals and turned right, away from the passage that led to the boiler itself. It took her an infinity before she finally reached what looked like a safe spot, a pile of what was probably old Mithraic habits—the cloth smelled of chalk and teacher-sweat, her nose giving her a jumble of impressions of round faces, bad food, and voices raised in a chorus of piercing sweetness.

Ruby sank down, curled into a ball, hugged her schoolbag close, and finally, gratefully, passed out.

THIRTY-FOUR

RUNNING, *WET BRANCHES SLAPPING HER FACE, A STITCH sinking its claws deep into her side. Behind her, the low whooshing as a sharp blade cleaved air. It was coming, its face a blankness, its shape hulking-wrong. The old nursery rhyme filled her skull—*

> Gaston hunts with stave and an axe,
> watch out, watch out or he'll claw your backs,
> olly-olly-oh, olly-olly-aye,
> one two three four! Time to die!

Then the ring of chanting children would spin faster and faster until someone tumbled, and they would all fall down, shrieking with laughter.

Kin didn't play that game, though. She'd seen it at primary school and sung the rhyme at home for Gran, who had just looked sour for a moment before saying, gently but inflexibly, We don't sing that here, Ruby.

Slipping in mud, a grating shock against her knees as she fell, back up in a flash and running, but she was tired and he was so fast, so fast. Darkness everywhere, the only faint gleams from falling raindrops or her own white hands, fluttering like birds as she ran, ran, ran.

A terrific, painless blow against her back. Warm dribbling down her chin.

She was still trying to run when she hit the ground, face-first in the leaves and the mud, and the pain came, a great cresting wave of it, breaking over her in starlight-streaked foam, and the claws came next, ripping as he tore her sideways, flipping her face-up and the sky was black. Against that blackness there were two small golden lamps, bad-luck eyes that would have been beautiful if not for the emptiness behind them, an emptiness nothing would ever fill.

The axeblade glinted as he lifted it high, and with a heaving snort, he chopped—

—down off the stack of black cloth, her breath hitching in to scream before she realized where she was and that she had to be *quiet*, for Mithrus's sake. She caught herself on hands and knees, and was up in a flash, her heart thumping so quickly the individual beats blurred together, a song of hideous fear.

Stacks of antique Mithrusmas decorations, masses of old textbooks, boxes with cryptic dates and abbreviations on the side under thick layers of dust and cobwebs. Her head rang, aching a little, and her nose was full. She sniffed several times, but all she got was dust. And her eyes were all crusty, *eww*. It was the kind of feeling you got after you'd cried yourself to sleep and then woke up late.

What time is it? She didn't even have a watch.

Ellie would have had a watch. She was always so *prepared.*

Ruby took stock. Grabbing her schoolbag hadn't been a bad idea, even if her French textbook weighed a ton. For one thing, her wallet was in there, so she had her student ID and leftover shopping money as well as charmed tinfoil, some breath mints—her stomach growled—and a pack of choco beechgum, which would calm her tummy down while she figured out what to do.

How long had she slept? There was the same dim glow in here as when she'd collapsed, from a bare bulb burning down the long passage, lighting the way to the boiler. It was also much warmer, almost stuffy, and she rubbed at her face again, wishing she'd been able to manage a warm shower. She should have taken off her shoes and socks to let them dry, too. Her feet felt swollen.

What would Ellie do?

Well, Ellie would have a simple elegant solution for finding out the time. Probably a charm, since she was just slopping over with Potential. Cami would probably just *know* what time it was, the way she seemed to just know how to do everything else.

At least they weren't involved in this huge mess. She'd kept them safely out of it. If they'd come in to meet Conrad yesterday . . .

. . . well, best not to even think about that. There were all *sorts* of things not to think about, and if she was going to decide what to do, she needed to, well, not dwell on them. Right?

But what if . . . he knew she had friends. Now she cursed herself for talking about them all the time; he could probably recognize them in a crowd if he had to. Not to mention they might be worried about her, if they weren't too busy with Nico and Avery and their lives going so smoothly. Maybe, just maybe, they would drop by the cottage, and if Conrad was there . . . he could be charming. He could be *really* charming. They might not see the danger until too late.

You're my way out.

Would she be able to make him stop, if she was collared? If she was collared, Gran wouldn't have to worry, and maybe by being quiet and pliable she wouldn't set Conrad off.

She eased herself back up on the pile of habits and took a deep breath. It was something to consider. If she could just stop being an irritant to everyone, a—

—*a selfish bitch, go on, admit it*—

—okay, fine, a selfish bitch, maybe it would fix things.

Except.

There was Hunter's body, wrapped in linen and lowered, fetching up against cold earth with that stomach-unseating little bump. And the girls—redheads. Mere-human.

All four, *dead*.

Even if she stopped Conrad doing . . . whatever it was he thought he was doing, that wouldn't be enough. Not if Thorne was blamed for everything, not even if Conrad stopped . . .

Stopped *killing*.

You could hunt, you could *find*, but kin didn't kill. Not unless you desperately needed food, but still, you took animals, and brought them home for cooking to prove you hadn't done something you shouldn't. You didn't kill mere-humans. Or other kin. It just . . . you just didn't do it.

It was *taboo*.

And . . . and Thorne would get blamed, and nobody would believe him, maybe because he was an only, maybe because he'd always been difficult. Thorny, so to speak.

It wasn't *fair*.

The same old stubborn resistance rose up in her. Like when Cami had been teased so relentlessly about her stutter in primary school, and Ruby had waded into the fray. Or Ellie, in middle school, new in town and mercilessly hassled. It wasn't *fair*, and that just lit every fuse in Ruby's head.

But what should she *do*? Ellie was the one with all the plans, Ruby just sort of waited to be given a task, or waited until someone like Binksy Malone opened her stupid mouth so Rube could jump on her.

Well, first she should probably find out what time it was. If she snuck up to the hall, she could probably peer out without getting caught. If she was careful.

She wasn't in her uniform, either. It was going to be tricky if she wanted to leave before school got out.

The rest, she decided, could wait until she'd found something to eat.

THIRTY-FIVE

SHE DIDN'T HAVE TO WORRY ABOUT BEING CAUGHT. The hall was dark and quiet, and for a few seconds she was confused, thinking she hadn't slept at all, before she realized she'd slept almost a whole *day*. No wonder she was hungry.

The clock above the lockers right next to Sister Margaret's classroom pointed at 7:48, and the entire bulk of St. Juno's held its breath. Not a sound in the whole place, even the soughing of the boiler—thank Mithrus whoever came down to check it hadn't found her—held behind a curtain of stillness. The urge to scream just because she could rose up, and for a minute the thought of running amok and doing every single prank she'd ever dreamed up in an entirely empty school held a certain attraction.

At home she'd be helping Gran wash up after dinner. Then more homework and Babchat before bed—but she hadn't been on Bab in a while, had she.

She blinked. The clock now pointed to 8:00. She'd just stood there staring at it for twelve whole minutes.

In that vacant inward time, she'd arrived at a conclusion.

She'd go to the hospital. If Gran was awake she could tell her everything. If not, she could find a Tante or Oncle and make them listen. If they wouldn't listen, she'd find another. *Someone* would be willing to believe Thorne wouldn't do these awful things.

Maybe even Detective Haelan. Now that she wasn't terrified and sleep deprived, she could think that maybe he'd be smart enough to see past Conrad's smile. And she could ask him more about her . . . mother. What she'd done that was so terrible kin wouldn't speak her name.

The first step was getting out of here. Then, finding transportation to Trueheart Memorial.

Ruby scraped her hair back, wincing as her fingers encountered tangles, and got moving.

The bus lurched around a corner, like a fat rolling silver sow, and Ruby braced herself against the swaying. There was a group of jacks in the back, sniggering about something or another, and the rest of the crowd was tired mere-humans, most of them probably coming home from work.

It was the jacks she kept an eye on while the bus lumbered, downshifting, up Trueheart Hill. They had bright bandannas tied at ankle, wrist, or knee—gang colors. One of them, a dark-haired boy with bone spurs on his weeping-slick cheeks, stared over the heads of everyone in the seats, and every time Ruby stole a glance in her peripheral vision he was looking right at her. He looked vaguely familiar as well, but she couldn't place him.

She had to stand, shifting from foot to foot and hanging on to a pole. Being on her feet seemed like a great idea, but it also meant the group at the back could see her.

Across the aisle, a stout graying man with a three-piece suit and a monocle glanced up from his newspaper, incuriously. The headline screamed at her in heavy dark print.

REDHEAD RIPPER STRIKES AGAIN.

The subtitle was chilling. *Four Slain, Killer at Large.* The type underneath wriggled and blurred: she couldn't read it at this distance. Four? Were they counting Hunter, or not?

There was a grainy picture, the top of a head with curly hair, but she couldn't see the rest of it under the fold. Why was he doing it? If he wanted to kill a redhead, why not Ruby?

What would happen if he *had* managed to get the collar on her?

She turned to peer out the window and realized the bus was three blocks from the hospital. The stop line almost burned her hands, but she yanked it and saw the sign at the front light up. *Stop Requested.*

The jacks in the back made a little more noise. She hoped

this wasn't their stop too and began pushing for the front door as the bus braked.

It was raining again, a thin penetrating drizzle, and the towered pile of the hospital crouched restlessly under the lashing wind. A Mithraic *tau* knot over the front doors was lit by a random reflection of headlights, and it actually cheered her up a little. It was like seeing the *tau* and the Magdalen's sad gaze all over St. Juno's, a secret little letter from the past.

Inside, the fluorescents and the reek of disinfectant and illness was just the same. Did time ever move in a hospital, or did it just slosh around aimlessly? Did it boil down thicker and thicker, the way Gran made candy sometimes?

Stop it. Pay attention.

She took the stairs instead of the elevator, even though her legs ached. Her trainers still squooshed a little. Her nose tingled, though, working just fine, leading her unerringly through the corridors and stairwells until she reached the private rooms. Spendy, but Woodsdowne could afford it, and the Clanmother would get the best of care.

If Gran was in the private rooms, she was out of critical care, and that was good, right?

Ruby ghosted past the nurse's station—there was nobody there, though voices echoed from a doorway leading into another space, where she could see the edge of locked glass-fronted cabinets and a long counter. Probably where they hid the dangerous drugs; two nurses murmuring like birds in the treetops. A sharp high note of laughter, and Ruby's nose twitched a little.

Even here, amid the disinfectant and boiled food and industrial laundry smells, she could trace Gran's familiar musk with its sharp undertone, the Levarin cologne she dabbed behind her ears and on her wrists with its layer of crushed green grass, and the faint odor of baking bread, warm fur, and safety. Ruby glanced in either direction, pressed down the door handle, and stepped inside a pale-pink seashell of a room that tried to be restrained and elegant under the clutter of medical paraphernalia. An IV pole, and a soft beeping from a monitor showing a heartbeat, nice and strong.

The window looked into a dark courtyard, three old thick-trunked oak trees beginning to drop their leaves in clumps to the stone walks below. Their branches scraped and rustled, almost audible through the rain-spattered glass.

Gran lay on the bed, its upper half tilted upward probably so she could breathe more easily. Thin tubes ran to her nose, and the pale fluid inside the IV sack, dangling overhead, dripped once, twice.

Ruby took a step forward.

It looked like she was sleeping. Her color was good, a high rosy blush on her planed-down cheeks, but her platinum hair was a little askew, its braid done by someone who lacked the requisite quick, firm fingers.

Sometimes Ruby braided Gran's hair. Gran said she was the best at it.

A small sound escaped Ruby's lips. Sleeping was good, right? She looked good. She looked, as a matter of fact, like she was just napping and would rise, irritated and brisk, setting everything to rights about her with quick efficiency.

There was a chair on the other side of the bed. Ruby pulled it close, and was just about to sink down when Gran's eyes snapped open.

Icy gray, her pupils pinpricks, the old woman stared straight ahead. Her thin lips moved, just a little, and the croak that came out froze Ruby clear through.

"Katrina?" Slurred, as if Gran had been at the whiskey too much and was pleasantly buzzed. "Katy, is that you?"

Ruby's breath rode a shuddering sleigh out of her mouth. "It's me, Gran." She reached for the old woman's hand, so fragile and bruised, and picked it up carefully. "I'm here."

"I did not mean to," Gran's voice sharpened, losing its slur, but she didn't blink. The fixed stare was a little . . . well, it was a little worrying, and Ruby's relief turned to ice trailing lightly down her back, little trickles of electricity. "I would not have . . . I burned the collar. I *burned* it. Why did you leave?"

Burned? It made no sense. "It's okay, Gran. It's okay."

"Forgive me . . . Katy, I would not have . . . I spoke in anger."

What? She patted Gran's hand, gently, trying not to touch

the heplock. It looked like a nasty growth on the back of Gran's familiar hand. "It's all right. It's okay."

"Forgive me . . . Katy, forgive me. . . ."

Ruby swallowed, hard. "I forgive you."

Gran's eyes slowly closed. She muttered and mumbled, falling back against the pillows, and her fingers were slack and cool.

There was no way Ruby could tell her anything. She was on her own.

Katy. *Katrina.* And a collar.

I burned it. Why did you leave?

Was this Katy alive somewhere else? Was that why she wasn't spoken of? Was she *taboo*? Had she just *left*?

You have other problems. Ruby exhaled, sharply. Gran was still sick. She was alive, and talking, but she wasn't . . . well, she wasn't *herself.*

Which meant Ruby was the only rootfamily who could give orders at the moment. She didn't have Gran's iron will, though. The Oncles would probably just laugh at her.

Then you wipe that laugh right off their faces, Ruby. You've got to. But *how*?

Her shoulders slumped, her schoolbag sagging against her. She hesitated, halfway between sinking into the chair and standing up, her thighs aching and every inch of her crawling with fear-residue and air-dried rain.

Imagine you're Gran. Imagine you're Ellie. Imagine you're anyone, just get it done.

She laid Gran's hand back down, ever so gently. "Okay. You . . . you rest and get better, Gran. I'm going to fix things."

How, I have no idea. But I'm gonna.

A few moments later, the room was empty, except for the old woman's steady breathing.

THIRTY-SIX

HEAD HELD HIGH, SHE SWEPT DOWN THE CORRIDOR and braced herself. If Gran was down here, there was probably a waiting room somewhere, and her nose told her there were kin about, musk and the aroma of dark, comforting Woodsdowne earth.

Further down the hall, opposite the nurse's station, was a collection of chairs welded together with tables too small to do anything but rest a tabloid on, a fishtank full of brightly colored ambulatory sushi, bright glaring light, and a half-dozen kin. Ruby stopped dead, nostrils flaring, her greeting dying in her throat. The choco beechgum turned to ash, and she almost swallowed it.

Oncle Efraim, his mouth a thin line as usual, had his head in his hands. All the kin present were male—a couple of the older cousins, Brent and Jackson Beaudry, and the tall, laconic Oncle Vidalis, his silver-sprinkled hair slicked down with rainwater.

Old Oncle Dean, and Oncle Tach, and a few more, the heads of the major branchfamilies.

Sitting right next to Efraim, with his hand solicitously on the older kin's shoulder, leaning in to murmur what could have been condolences, was Conrad Tiercey. He looked just the same, in a white T-shirt and jeans, his boots worn in by now and freshly brushed, and the clan cuff on his wrist had continued to rub. The rash had spread halfway up his forearm, and it looked painful.

Ruby ducked aside, hoping the angle of the wall would hide her. Conrad was *right there*, and it was a group of Oncles. Brent would be disposed to listen to her, maybe, and Oncle Tach always heard anyone out. But Efraim, who had once muttered that Wild girlkin should be collared to keep them from wandering as a matter of course? And Jackson, who had chased her like Thorne and Hunter for a while, until she'd embarrassed him in front of the whole clan at a barbeque? If it was a group of Tantes, it would be better, but it wasn't.

She didn't need a weathervane to see the way the wind would blow, with Conrad standing right there. Why was Oncle Efraim shaking his head? Where was Tante Sasha? She was head of her own branch, and so was Tante Jeanette.

Footsteps. A shadow in the door behind the nurse's counter, another low laugh. Someone would step out and see her standing right here, and probably sing out a *Hello there, can I help you?*

Kin

All the kin would look. Already Brent's head was up, and he took a cautious sniff, as if he could smell her, rain-dipped and dirty as she was.

At least I know where Conrad is. He's not at the cottage. He probably drove my car here.

Which meant she could go home, maybe pack some clothes, and take a look at that duffel bag of his. If there was any proof, she could bring it to the kin, especially the Tantes, and have it not be her word against a guest's.

It was a plan worthy of Ellie, but she didn't have time to congratulate herself. She took off down the hall, away from the nurse's station, toward the stairwell door.

A few seconds later, when the nurse on duty stepped out with a fresh cup of coffee and settled behind the counter with a stack of paperwork, glancing over the men in the waiting area with a practiced, compassionate eye, the stairwell door was already closed.

THIRTY-SEVEN

IT WAS NO GREAT TRICK TO FIND HER BABY IN THE underground parking lot. The extra key, in its charmsealed magnetic box under the back bumper, was gone, but her own keys were in her schoolbag where they belonged. A few minutes later, she pulled out onto Stiltskin Street, the Semprena running a little rougher than she liked but okay enough. There was a crumpled dent in the bonnet that filled her with weary anger. As fast as she drove, she'd never so much as nicked the car.

It is an heirloom, Gran's voice whispered in her memory, and now Ruby wondered just who had driven it before her.

The backseat was full of drive-through wrappers and damp clothing, and it reeked. She had to roll both windows down and breathe through her mouth, that rusted-red smoke and rot scent overlaying everything along with the fume of his rage making her eyes water. His anger had soaked into the *seats*, for God's sake, and there was a long rip down the passenger's seat, stuffing and springs poking out. He'd slashed it with something, she could just *see* it, his face that snarling mask as the blade cut. . . .

Had he been imagining someone sitting there? She squirmed uncomfortably at the thought. How had he trashed the car in so short a time? It was phenomenal.

It probably wasn't the best idea to stop in the driveway, but at least she *backed* in. She could be out of here in a hot second. Granted, she'd only thought of that after the garage-door opener hadn't worked for some reason, but better late than never. She couldn't be smart as Ellie, but at least she *learned*.

The drizzle was icy. You couldn't tell that a week ago it had been hot enough to roast turtles in the shade. She ran for the front door, her keys jangling, head down against the rain, but she needn't have worried with the keys. The doorknob turned easily, and as soon as she stepped inside she coughed, rackingly, her eyes watering afresh.

It smelled *awful*, and there was that terrible brassy depth to the reek she wouldn't have been able to place if she hadn't been in Woodsdowne Park yesterday. Was it only yesterday?

Oh, Mithrus. No.

She hesitated, torn between looking for the source of that smell or going up to the second floor to find something, anything, that could serve as proof.

It didn't matter, she realized as she raised her head and took another few nervous steps into the living room. The smell, as far as she could tell, was coming from upstairs.

The living room was a shambles. The tapestry had been torn down, the couches and overstuffed chairs sliced and shredded, Gran's careful arrangement of pictures and candlesticks on the mantel a shattered jumble on the stone hearth, her charming supplies scattered. Lamps knocked over—the curtains were drawn, probably to hide the state of the place.

Again, the scope of the damage he'd been able to cause in so short a time was nothing short of fantastic. Just thinking about how she would have to somehow clean it all up was exhausting.

For a moment, she stared at the fireplace's dark cavern. The metal screen, worked with enameled decorations—a hummingbird, a swan—had been pulled loose and lay crumpled under the front window. Gran's rocker was also smashed to flinders.

I burned it. . . . I spoke in anger. . . .

What had happened between Katrina and Gran? What had Gran burned?

Forgive me . . . forgive me. . . . Experimenting with live flame and a Beaudry's charm . . .

It didn't matter what Gran had been burning. She could think about it later.

Ruby eased for the stairs, moving quietly even though there was nobody here. At least her nose wasn't running, although it would be really nice if she didn't have those images of splayed limbs and brackish, rotting blood flashing through her head, along with . . .

She stopped, head upflung, on the stairs. Sniffed cautiously, little tiny sips through her nostrils to untangle every thread. A familiar musk, full of fierce silence and dark eyes, quick graceful movements and a coolness against her nape, a smell that filled her with unsteady, vaporous hope.

"Thorne?" she breathed, and ran up the stairs.

It was a faint fading thread, as if he'd been damping his scent like any kin could, and the upstairs was empty.

Well, mostly empty.

Her room hadn't been torn apart too badly. Her dresser had been rifled, and her mirror was broken, but that was it. Thorne had been here, too, but only briefly. She followed the thread of his scent to the spare room, bracing herself as the smell of death and rotting thickened, and peered in.

Thorne had spent a while in here. Had he been looking for proof too? Where had he been *hiding*? When kin wanted to find you, they *found* you, unless heavy-duty charm or fey was covering your tracks. Thorne wasn't a charmer, so . . .

The spare bed was made, neatly. Burnt-out candles stood in built-up wax everywhere, and the mirror over the dresser was starred with one large chunk of breakage, as if a fist had crunched into it but not shattered the glass completely. On the spare bed, with its dusky rose comforter, was Conrad's duffel bag, opened and ruthlessly scattered. Thorne's scent was very, very strong here, and if there was anything to find he probably would have found it.

Still, Ruby looked. An empty leather wallet caught her eye, amid the tangle of clothes. Two books, ripped to small shreds and impossible to identify, and a thin silver chain holding a fluidly twisted medallion.

The key to the collar. She grabbed that, stuffing it in her pocket as well, where it clicked against the lone luckcharm from her broken maryjanes.

She turned in a full circle. The dresser drawers were empty, the closet door half-ajar and showing a few lonely hangers. Nothing else.

Why hadn't he unpacked? He'd been here long enough. Or was he planning to leave, once he'd . . . once he'd what?

You're my way out!

She stood, hugging herself as drizzle beaded on the window. Thorne's scent was fresh. If she'd gotten here earlier, could she have caught him? Told him she believed it wasn't him? He was smart as Ellie, even if he was difficult; he'd have an idea or two. She wouldn't feel so . . . alone.

She shook herself, and checked the bathroom. Nothing in there, but the mirror was broken too. Had he broken *all* the glass?

Maybe he didn't want to look at himself.

Kin

The master bedroom at the end of the hall had a tightly closed door. Gran usually left it open; even as a child Ruby would rarely dare to step over the threshold unless invited. Gran wasn't mean, but she gave scrupulous privacy—and expected it in return. It was different at night, when the childhood terrors came.

Ruby twisted the knob, bracing herself.

There was no bracing for this.

The body lay on Gran's antique cherrywood bed with its high posts and red curtains. Opened up like a meat flower, white chips of bone showing through rent skin and torn muscle. Arranged as if sleeping, her dyed-red hair spread on Gran's crisp white pillows, her head turned to the side and the internal architecture of her neck bared because the skin was hanging in a loose flap over her chest. The remains of jeans and a bright red T-shirt, cheap cotton probably bought at a discount store, because the dye had bled onto her wet skin.

Ruby backed up, her hand clapped over her mouth. Gran's dresser stood closed and secretive as always, but the full-length mirror across from the antique spinning wheel lay in shards on the floor. The wheel, draped in sheer fabric to keep the dust off, hunched in the corner, Gran's old stool behind it. Sometimes, late at night when Ruby was very young, she would hear the hiss-thump of the wheel, just like a heartbeat.

Oh Mithrus, Mithrus please . . .

Dim alarm spilled through the roaring. It had come back, unwanted companion, filling up her head with static like the space between stations. What was that?

Car door slamming.

Someone was here.

THIRTY-EIGHT

SHE MADE IT TO HER ROOM JUST AS THE FRONT DOOR creaked open. The sound of breathing filled the cottage, or maybe it was just that her ears were straining past the roaring, past even a kin's sensitive hearing. Her window slid up, letting in a drench of chill night air laden with rain and the smell of wet leaves. Autumn filled her nose, the season of harvest.

Summer had lingered, but it was gone now.

"Don't." He was in the doorway. "Don't run."

She swallowed, hard. Turned from the window, balanced on her toes in case he came for her. Stared at him.

Conrad stood easily, feet braced, the collar dripping and twisting from his left hand. Some speckles of drizzle on his hair—it was longer than when he'd arrived at the train station, but just as black. His eyes were just as golden, and the faint shadow of stubble on his cheeks made him look just as sharply handsome and dangerous as ever.

Now Ruby could see the abyss behind those compelling, aching eyes.

Her throat was dry. "Why are you doing this?"

Now there was a flash of expression crossing his face. Puzzlement, perhaps, or pain. "I . . . you're . . ." A deep breath. "You're my way out, Ruby. When you're with me, *really* with me, I'll have everything." A slight twitch, the collar swinging, chiming flatly to itself. "We'll go away. To a different city, or into the Waste. You'll be perfect. Once we get this . . . this little thing done."

"You want to collar me and take me out into the *Waste*? Are you insane?" *Stupid question, Ruby. He's* obviously *insane.* "You've *killed* people! You've killed *kin!*"

"I *solved problems!*" he shouted. "I've solved *every* problem! Nobody's between us now! Nothing can stop us!"

"Nobody's between . . ." The roaring in her head got worse. Was that what he thought he was doing? Solving problems?

What had happened to the boy who *was* a problem, just like her?

"I was only going to stay the night. Each day I thought, well, today's the day they'll get news. But I couldn't leave. Because of *you.* You're beautiful, you're *perfect*, and you were meant to be his."

"Meant to be . . ." She couldn't get enough air in. That empty gaze swallowed everything, burrowed inside her head. "What? *Whose?*"

"I had a brother." He was moving forward, one slow step at a time. Her school uniform, still tangled on the floor, was crushed again under his boots. The rash spreading up from his clan cuff, angry red, had begun to weep a little. "He had everything first, and best."

"And always," she managed, remembering. How could the two of them—the boy who had hunched next to her on the front step and this . . . this *thing* . . . live in the same body? Why didn't it explode from the sheer incomprehensibility of its own existence?

"Until I solved that." Conrad took another step forward. He was at the end of her bed now. "And then I saw you." The collar jangled, musically. "You're *mine* now, and we'll be together. You want it, your grandmother wanted it—"

"How do you know?"

He actually stopped, cocking his head. Stared at her. "She wants what's best for you."

Ruby opened her mouth to reply, but there was a sound from downstairs. Her breath caught, her pulse jackrabbiting in her throat and wrists, ankles and temples, her entire body a shivering heartbeat.

"Mithrus Christ, look at this." Ellie's voice, a soft breath of wonder. "What the hell?"

"Ruby?" Cami, sounding worried. "*Ruby?* Are you here?"

"The pendulum says so." Ellie's footsteps crunched on something broken. "Careful, Cami."

"Ruby!" Cami's voice cracked halfway through the word, and Conrad's face distorted into a thick, congested snarl. The shift rippled through him, glossy black fur sprouting and muscles bulking, his tallness turning a little stooped as his spine lengthened. Except it was somehow *wrong*. Ruby had seen kinboys shift all her life, especially at fullmoon, but something in Conrad's slumping growth was off, and nausea slammed hard into her midriff.

"Problems," the beast growled, and he whirled with fluid grace. He bulleted out the door, taking a chunk of the wall out with one of his clawed hands as he spun.

Heading for the stairs. The downstairs.

And her helpless, vulnerable friends.

Not my friends, you bastard. Not . . . my . . . friends!

Ruby bolted after him. The shift burned inside her, silverglass spikes, and she realized she was snarling too, a low musical note of bloodlust.

THIRTY-NINE

HE WAS SO *FAST*.

She leapt from the top of the stairs, colliding with him half-way, the cracking of the rosewood banister lost in the noise they were both making. Rolling, the side of her head blooming with wet warm pain, his claws burning as they striped fire up her arm, and both of them fetched up in a tumbled heap at the bottom.

He shook off the daze first, his sleek head snaking back and forth as he rolled to his feet. The sound he was making scraped over Ruby's skin, sandpaper fury and wirebrush rage, and Ca-mi's scream was lost under the scratching, roaring rumble.

Ruby fish-jumped, her entire body exploding up from the floor. She sidled a few steps, the wrecked living room opening up behind her, and didn't have any time to reassure her friends or say anything, because Conrad was already streaking forward.

Besides, the shift was burning all the way through Ruby, a

glow no longer silver but red as sunset. Bones shifted, her skin twitching madly, kingirls didn't get furry like boys did. But the claws were just as sharp, the teeth were just as white, the eyes just as keen—and the hide just as tough.

She backhanded the Conrad-thing, a jolt smashing all the way through her. He was *heavy*. If he'd been regular kin she could have tossed him all the way back into the wall.

He wasn't. She didn't have time to think about why he was so much stronger, because he only slid back a few feet.

There was a popping zing, a crackle, and a bolt of blue-white arced from behind Ruby, splashing against Conrad's hide. Smoke and steam rose, a horrible scent of roasting, and under the flayed jeans—he was shifted so far even his clothes were bursting—and torn T-shirt Ruby could see boiling blisters erupt.

Looked like Ellie had enough presence of mind to throw a charm or two. Which was good, it was flat-out *great*, but if her aim was off she could fry Ruby just as well.

Doesn't matter. She coiled herself, sinking down, palms slapping the hardwood floor and her claws slicing like an iron knife through pale feybutter.

He snarled, and she snarled back, both deep grinding noises.

His said, *I will kill.*

Hers replied, *I am rootkin, and you will not have my friends.*

Could he understand that? Or was his mind, just like hers, a

Kin

wasteland now, the low umber and charcoal of a forest fire's aftermath, glowing coals and sparks still plenty capable of burning but nothing even approaching a coherent thought?

She knew only that she had to protect.

He scrabbled forward slightly, and she responded, sidling again. Couldn't afford to circle, they were behind her, if she could drive him out the door and—

He sprang, claws grinding as he launched himself, and Ruby uncoiled a half-second later. Her claws went in, piercing hide and grating against ribs, and she pulled him down from the height of his leap, crashing into the couch. More smoking, roasting smell, he clawed at her, bloodscent rising. Stripes of fire along the outside of her leg, her cheek, she kept twisting so he couldn't hook into her guts and splash them all over the floor.

Get out get out—

If they ran, she could keep him occupied long enough for them to escape. It was worth it.

A terrific smashing. The wreck of a chair, brought down across the Conrad-thing's back. A flash of Cami, blue eyes glowing and her canines lengthened into sweet, wicked little fangs, her face a mask of effort as she grabbed another sharp chunk of the coffee table, lifting it high.

Ellie, her platinum hair rising on a breeze from nowhere and her hands alive with silver-spitting charmlight, tossed a complex, flashing charmsphere straight into Conrad's face. It burst, and blood burst with it, spattering Ruby as she squirmed desperately, her claws slicing deep in his hide.

He bellowed, a massive wall of sound, and Ruby was the only one who could hear the agony in that cry, the boy behind the monster.

She rose from the remains of the couch, shaking him off like water, and kicked him. He curled around the force of the kick, sliding back along the floor, and fetched up against the fireplace's bottom with a sickening crack.

Run! She wanted to yell it, but her mouth was full of sharp teeth, her jaw the wrong shape for speaking. She snapped a glance at the two girls, Cami holding the heavy chunk of oak table aloft like an ink-haired barbarian princess in a rumpled St. Juno's uniform, beautiful and wild. Ellie's eyes were wide and silvery, and Potential sparks flashed in an odd pattern over her head, her platinum hair ruffling on her own personal breeze as her lips moved slightly, her long fingers spinning out threads of Potential.

They were so beautiful it made her heart hurt.

"Ruby look out—" Cami's scream, choked off as something hit Ruby, *hard*, the wall smashing behind her. Red, pulsing unconsciousness swallowed her whole.

All the pinches, the squeezes, the little insults masquerading as affection. Taking her car. Putting the backpack in Thorne's room. Holding Oncle Efraim's shoulder as if he was true kin, as if he was a help and support.

Kin

And the *bodies*. Girls he didn't even *know*, and how had he gotten them into the woods? Just torn up and discarded.

Because of me.

What happened next was a confused jumble. Snarling rage, the shift a sweet wine-red pain all through her, the world turning over and her bones full of flame. Shattering glass, the crackle of live Potential as Ellie screamed something, everything around Ruby smearing like ink on wet paper.

She bulleted through the gaping hole that used to be the front window, into thin fine soaking drizzle. The curtains, shredded by whatever had happened, flirted unsteadily on a cold breeze full of blood, anger, and the exhalation of an autumn night on the cusp of fullmoon.

A long trail of bloodspatter ended at a horrible, uneven shape.

FORTY

THE CONRAD-THING SNARLED, NOWHERE NEAR BASE-
form or shift, now. It was a black hulking thing, its paws having lost opposable thumbs and its mad golden eyes still terribly
empty. It favored its left front paw, blood dripping from its thick
pelt, its hide steaming and scorched.

It was what the Tantes and Oncles warned of, why they
helped with the shift when you were young. Why you didn't do
taboo things, even if you were Wild. The Moon's gifts had teeth
and claws, and if you did not use them well, She would take Her
blessings back.

With interest.

The shift fell away from Ruby, the hurts and claw-marks
healing as it retreated. Her T-shirt flapped, sticky with cooling
blood. Her own, and . . . and his.

The smoke had swallowed his smell. Red and ash, burning
blood, a reek that meant *taboo*. He'd gone too far into the shift.

He'd become what the Wolfhunters thought kin always were—mindless appetite, destruction, revenge.

Did I do that? She stared at the thing. *Mithrus Christ.*

"Ruby!" Cami, scrambling through the hole behind her. "Look out! He's—"

"It's okay," Ruby heard herself say, dully. She'd been far gone in the shift herself, and she could have killed him.

She could even do it now. She could let the rage take her, all the hurt and pain and frustration and fear, and she'd be unstoppable. For all Conrad's bigger size and greater weight, he just didn't *get* that she was the dangerous one.

Because she wouldn't just kill him. She'd tear his body apart like he'd torn up those girls, and Hunter.

And then she would be what he was.

For a bare second she trembled on the edge of it, her gaze clear and steady, locked with the twin gold-ringed holes that were the beast's eyes.

She could be exactly like that.

"Careful. Broken glass." Ellie, practical as ever, a thin-thread whisper over the buzz and crackle of Potential. "I think he's getting ready to tango again."

"It's fine," Ruby murmured. The dominance in her swelled. It held the beast pinned, like a butterfly on a specimen board. Cami had cried during that Science class at Havenvale, when Mr. Rambling had explained the killing jar and the pins through gem-bright wings, and Ruby had given Binksy Malone a filthy look when the bitch sniggered.

She'd shut Binksy *right* up, thank Mithrus.

The memory helped, a little. There were others crowding inside her—Cami, pale and barely breathing on a hospital bed until a silver medallion was torn away. Cami sobbing in her arms, while she and Ellie held her and tried their best to soothe.

Ellie on the staircase of a slumping, sliding house, turning away from the spider-shadowed thing above her, the thing that had almost robbed Ruby of her friend. And finally, Ellie hanging between her and Cami like wet washing, sobbing *Let me go,* and Ruby's own reply, ringing inside her like only the truth could.

Not now, not ever.

They'd come here to find her. They hadn't hesitated at all, just leapt in on her behalf, just like she'd always jumped in on theirs.

They'd seen her shift, too.

The Conrad-thing strained, lunging against Ruby's will. But there were other sounds in the dark now, too. Whispers and movement, and other gleams of eyes.

Woodsdowne kin melted out of the shadows, leaping the low stone wall around Gran's garden, flowing around the corners of the house, clambering over the roof and dropping down to land with soft authority. There was Oncle Efraim and Tante

Kin

June and Tante Sasha, and Brent and Carissa and Harper and Joel, Oncle Zech and Oncle Tod and Oncle Barry and others. There was Hunter's mother, Tante Alissa, her lip lifted in a snarl as she scented the foulness that was the creature.

And there was Thorne, wet clear through, his dark gaze fierce and hot, his hair slicked down. He'd lost weight, but it just made the essential fire in him shine so much brighter.

He was alive.

The relief that hit her made her stagger, and her hold on the thing slipped a fraction. It scrabbled, but it was too late. The Oncles descended on him, snarling, but it was the Tantes who ripped his limbs free with heaving cracks, giving mercy as only the Moon's daughters could. They *gave* life, like the Moon—so that mercy was theirs to give, and they granted it.

The cousins clustered around, a solid wall blocking the awful sight, their voices lifted in savage song.

Later, she heard that when they ripped the clan cuff away, the rash turned out to be from a long, thin spiraling wound on his wrist. As if he'd wrapped a thin jangling silver thing around and around it, and pulled the clan cuff tight enough to make the collar cut his skin.

Ruby sagged. Thorne was still coming, stepping through the hollyhocks, crushing the dying marigolds, paying no attention to the rosebushes, just walking right through them, straight for her.

But it was Ellie who grabbed Ruby and spun her around. She shook her, once, twice, *hard*. Then Ruby was enveloped in a hug full of ice and wildness, Potential and Ellie's peculiar blue-tinged smell, sort of like the scented markers they gave you in fourth grade.

Cami flung her arms around them both, and it was her preternatural strength that kept them upright when Ruby's legs turned to noodles. She crumpled, and they held her in the rain, Thorne hovering anxiously an arm's-length away, smelling of worry and cinders.

The dam inside her broke again, and Ruby began to sob.

FORTY-ONE

THIS BLUE-WALLED ROOM IN THE FLETCHER CHARM-clan mansion was familiar, if only because little marks of El-lie's personality were scattered all through it, from the shelf of heavy-duty tomes on charming theory to the cerulean scarves draped over the headboard of the wide, soft bed.

"It was Thorne." Cami hovered near the small, obviously antique, white-painted vanity, watching Ruby's face, anxiously. Her skin glowed in the warm golden light, and there was no trace of the sharp canines she'd shown earlier.

Ellie rubbed at Ruby's hair with the towel, gentle and brisk. "It was kind of a shock to get a call from him, and he was so furious nothing made much sense. Livvie did some locate-charming—"

"Only because you were going to do it yourself if I didn't." Livvie Fletcher, Avery's mother, folded her arms and gave Ellie a stern look. When she did that, you could see that she was older, and you could also see an echo of Avery in her high cheekbones and soft dark hair with its stubborn curl over her forehead. "Though I couldn't get a lock on Ruby until this evening. Which distresses me."

"I was hiding," Ruby said blankly. *In Juno's boiler room.* Nobody could have found her behind those walls.

She tried not to look in the mirror. She'd never shifted in front of them before, and uneasy relief warred with fresh worry. Ellie had shoved her into the scrubbed-clean white bathroom, and a hot shower would have been heavenly, except Ruby cried, softly, all through it. Not sobbing, just . . . leaking. Again.

"Hiding so well none of our clan could find you?" Mrs. Fletcher's tone was a question, but she didn't push. "Ellie took the charm-pendulum when it started twitching."

"I stole it," Ellie supplied, almost cheerfully. "I knew something bad was going to happen, and I left a note. But I suspect I'm grounded for it."

"We'll talk about that later. Avery's furious you didn't take him."

"He was asleep. He was out all night looking for Rube." Ellie didn't look like the prospect of being grounded filled her with dread. She started combing Ruby's wet hair with gentle, efficient strokes. "Cami picked me up, and we just followed the pendulum. It's a good thing, too."

"I'm sor—" Ruby began immediately, but Ellie tugged at her hair. Very gently.

"Stop that. Why didn't you say something? We knew something wasn't right, but you wouldn't *talk*." Ellie's eyebrows had drawn together, and she looked almost fierce.

"F-for a change." Cami shrugged when Ellie rolled her eyes. "Do you know how s-scary that was?"

Ruby hunched her shoulders. "I was trying . . . Gran wanted me to be . . . different."

"Are you kidding? She's so proud of you." Ellie finished combing, stepped back to examine her work, and nodded once. "Okay, let's get you some clothes. You can't go anywhere in a bathrobe." She bounded away, across the room, toward a cherrywood wardrobe that looked big enough to hide a small country in.

"It probably wouldn't matter," Ruby muttered.

Livvie Fletcher's gaze was kind, and worried as Gran's sometimes was. "Your uncle—Efraim, I think? He's downstairs waiting to take you to the hospital. That's where Thorne is, I gather. He's a nice boy, very polite."

Since when? She hadn't had a chance to talk to him—they had whisked her away, Cami piloting the Spyder through slackening rain while Ellie huddled in the back with Ruby, hugging so hard Ruby could barely breathe.

I need to go home, she'd moaned, empty of everything but shock and the idea that she had to start cleaning up.

No you don't, Ellie had replied, fiercely. *You need help, and you're going to get it. Don't argue.*

"Ruby?" Cami, shyly. "C-can you . . . what *was* that?"

That was the question she'd been dreading. "Conrad," she whispered. Even the name raised gooseflesh on her arms, under the soft, comfortable indigo bathrobe that smelled of Ellie and comfort. "He . . . he was sick. *Taboo*. He . . ."

"Don't." Mrs Fletcher was suddenly right next to her. She bent down, and the hug was awkward even though Ruby could tell she meant to help. "Now isn't the time. I'm going to go tell your uncle you're getting ready. The police will be at the hospital. You're going to be all right, Ruby."

Ruby nodded, and the silence that fell when Livvie Fletcher left was full of awkward edges.

"Thank Mithrus." Ellie grabbed a handful of clothes. "Cami, you want something to wear? That's all wet."

"I'm f-fine." The Vultusino girl wouldn't look away from Ruby's face, which felt strange. Twitchy, as if she was shifting. "I've n-never seen you l-like that, Ruby."

Ruby shut her eyes. Of course. What were they going to—

"Me neither." Ellie padded toward her. "It was *beautiful*. I mean, scary as fuck, but beautiful."

"Gorgeous," Cami said firmly, and when Ruby opened her eyes she met Cami's blue gaze squarely. "I loved the way your eyes glowed. Don't you ever d-do that again, R-Ruby. We were scared. W k-kept trying to figure out how to help you—"

"She was trying to protect us." Ellie, matter of fact, held up a thick black jumper. "I'd loan you panties, but that is just . . . well, I mean, unless you absolutely need—"

Kin

Ruby's mouth twitched. A slow, delighted grin spread across Cami's face.

It was no use. She couldn't hold back the laughter. It spilled out, a little screamy and breathless, but with her friends laughing too, you couldn't hear it, even with a kin's ears.

All you could hear was love.

PART V:

THE WOODSMAN

FORTY-TWO

THE WAITING ROOM SEEMED A LITTLE SMALLER NOW. Ruby hunched, still shivering even though she was in dry clothes and Thorne's jacket was draped over her shoulders. The chair was hard and uncomfortable, but she was dry, at least. There was no way one of Ell's bras would fit her, but there was a soft cashmere jumper and jeans that should have been a little snug, but weren't because Ruby was thinner.

When had that happened?

"Adam Tiercey." Thorne was right next to her, perched on a chair just like hers. The fishtank burbled, and the nurses were giving them some odd looks.

Of course the rest of the waiting area was jammed with kin, Oncles and Tantes, and most of them looked angry. All of them were spotted with rain, and though the nurses probably couldn't smell the blood, something deep and atavistic might have been warning them.

Ruby stared at the carpet between her feet. She felt exhausted. Hollowed out.

Ell even had a pair of trainers that fit her, and dry socks. Her feet still felt damp, though. "Is that his name?"

"Yeah. Rootfamily. Conrad's twin, the younger one." Thorne's hand twitched, as if he wanted to touch her. Between them was a tiny little table holding two ancient yellowed magazines, both with grinning housewives on the cover. "He turned out to be a little . . . unsteady."

"I guess." She blinked, exhaustion turning everything into a leaden, unsurprising soup. Cami had to go home, and Ell was probably at this moment being read the riot act for getting into another crazy-dangerous situation. "How did . . ."

"Clanmother suspected something off when he showed up without a sub to clean his boots. She and that detective—Haelan—"

That managed to rouse her. "I told him it wasn't you."

"What?"

"I told him there was no way you would have done anything like that." She didn't look up, but she could feel his gaze on her. He leaned over a little farther. If he kept going like that, he'd probably end up on the teensy table between them.

"Oh." He cleared his throat. "Anyway, Haelan took me to the train station. Clanmother gave me a ticket to New Avalon. I went to go find out, she wanted it done quietly. And I think she wanted me out of the way."

Maybe. Or she wanted you not to show up dead in the Park, too. "You went all the way to New Avalon?"

"Just told you I did." He let out a sharp breath, almost a sigh. "Found out Adam and Conrad boarded the train together. Nobody's heard from Conrad since. One of the conductors remembered a pair of guys at the Vairshall station, about halfway between here and New Avalon. Said one guy looked like he was drunk, and they went into the station house. Grimtree's Clanmother sent a few of their cousins up there, they got off in Vairshall and looked around. Funny thing was, Adam was collared to keep him stable, they also thought some of our kin might be able to help him, teach him how to control himself. Wonder how he got it off." He paused. "You . . . you want some coffee? Something to eat? You're pretty pale."

There are probably all sorts of ways to take a collar off. On a train, there would be no place for the real Conrad to hide the key. Or if he was buzzy on liquor, or asleep, maybe he hadn't kept track of it as well as he could? Or maybe he'd been talked into taking the collar off for just a few minutes, because they were brothers, after all. . . .

She shook her head slightly. She'd probably never know. "You came back on the train. When?"

"Just got in, actually. Oncle Efraim met me at the station, told me Clanmother was sick, then it all made sense."

"What did?"

"Well . . . they found Conrad. The real Conrad, I mean."

291

Murmurs of conversation around them. Tante Alissa kept glancing over at Thorne, a line between her eyebrows. Had she believed him responsible for Hunter's . . . death?

Her throat was dry. "They . . . found him?"

"Yeah. He'd been stuffed in a dustbin about two blocks from the station, probably hadn't been opened since the Reeve. The lock was torn off. His body . . . well, he'd been poisoned."

"Poisoned?" She dropped her head forward again, because Oncle Efraim was looking at her. His mouth was thin, turned down at the corners. He hadn't said a word the whole way here.

"Aconite." Thorne's fingers twisted together.

But that's . . . "Wolfsbane," she heard herself say, and a laugh bubbled up in her throat. Died away on a tide of sourness. "We can't smell it as well." *It'd be easy to slip in a drink. Or train food, it's supposed to be nasty. Then he could take the key and* . . . She shuddered.

"Yeah. Tox screens came back positive for it, so the Grimtree Clanmother started calling around down here. Adam had been calling as both of them, I guess he was pretty good at it. Mimicking his brother. According to them, everything was just fine, but then . . . silence. She finally got Oncle Zech on the wire, and things started to come together. So when I got back there was the good old detective waiting for me with Oncle Efraim, and a couple cousins too. They told me you'd disappeared." He cleared his throat again, harshly. "I, uh, I went a little crazy."

"Uh-huh." She hunched her shoulders.

"I had to make sure you were safe. I couldn't believe they'd . . ." A deep breath. "So I called your friends, trying to find you. Nothing. I went to the Clanmother's looking for you, or for your trail, or anything. He was gone, but I found his ID in his wallet. And there was something under his bed. A hachet. Silver chasing on the . . . on the blade."

Her gorge rose, briefly, pointlessly. *Oh, God.* "That's what he used on the . . ." *The girls. Mithrus. And Hunter, that was why the body was . . . scorched.*

"Yeah."

A long silence stretched between them. Everything made sense now. Finally, Ruby wet her dry lips, a quick nervous flutter of her tongue. "I'm sorry."

"*You* didn't do anything." He sounded baffled, and he leaned over a bit more. He was going to fall out of the chair if this kept up. "The reason I went to the Clanmother in the first place was because of . . . of Hunter."

"Hunter," she repeated, to keep him talking. Her arm muscles twitched a little, burnt out. Even though the cuts and clawmarks had healed, there was still a deep ache left behind everywhere the thing had managed to get her.

"Hunt swore up and down that it wasn't the real Conrad, that it was probably his twin. He said he remembered both of them, even that long ago, and Hunt just *knew*. He was absolutely certain, and I brushed it off. Told him he just didn't like competition. He . . . I think he went to meet this Adam guy in the Park and . . . Ruby."

He slid off his seat and was on his knees in front of her. He had her hands, lying limp and discarded in her lap, and peered up into her face, her hair brushing his forehead and cheeks.

This close, she could see the circles under his eyes, and the piercing of his gaze had grown more intense, if that was possible. "It was my fault." Low, and fierce. "I'm sorry. I'm so goddamn sorry. If I'd believed Hunt, none of this would have happened. He'd be alive, and you'd be safe, and . . . I just didn't . . . Ruby, I'm sorry. You're not ever gonna forgive me. I know that, I'm okay with it, I just . . . I wanted to say I'm sorry."

The massive injustice of it stung her, giving her a small flush of energy. "It's not your fault." Her hands came back to life, grabbed his, and *squeezed*. "Don't you *dare* blame yourself. I covered for Conra—for whoever he was. I thought Hunter was maybe waiting in the Park for me to sneak out. I kept my mouth shut every time Conr—*Adam* did anything. I should have seen everything before."

"Don't—"

She squeezed his hands harder. "Then *you* don't, either. Okay?"

"I . . ." His face squinched up, as if he was eleven again. "I thought he made you happy, maybe. I would have challenged him in the open, if . . . but then I thought maybe you liked him, or . . . I just . . . I wanted you safe. And I was jealous too. I've always . . . Ruby, I just . . ."

"I know." She leaned forward with a weary sigh, and her forehead bumped gently against his. His breath was a little sour, but so was hers, and her hair fell down, closing both of them in their own private world. "I thought Gran wanted me to pick him. I wanted to be what she wants, but I'm not."

"Are you kidding? Every time she talks about you, it's that you're amazing. She's so proud of you, Rube. So proud." His throat worked as he swallowed. His eyes were closed. "I am too. You just . . . you were there in the garden, all lit up and angry and . . . and beautiful." She shook her head a little, but he pressed on. "Don't. You're everything anyone could ever want, Rube. If the Clanmother doesn't know it, *I'll* tell her so. I'll make her listen, too."

No wonder Gran had collapsed. Aconite. Now that they knew, could they treat her?

Would she be okay?

She untangled herself from Thorne, gently. He stared up at her, and the naked hope and longing on his face was almost too much to stand.

Deep down, she'd known all along he was the one. What would happen now?

I don't know.

"Miss de Varre?" A familiar voice. She'd guessed he would probably show up.

FORTY-THREE

SHE SMOOTHED HER FINGERS OVER THORNE'S FORE-head. He leaned into the touch, and when she looked up, she was afraid the lump in her throat would stop her from speaking.

It didn't, though. "Detective Haelan."

He was just as gray and rumpled and sad as ever. Still, the sharp intelligence in his eyes asked for—and gave—no quarter. "I think we should talk."

"I do too." She pulled, and Thorne rose. He also steadied her as she stood, her legs protesting wearily. "I told you he didn't do it."

"I knew he didn't. Hell of an alibi. It was also too neat, the backpack showing up." He sighed, and didn't seem to notice that the assembled kin had gone quiet, staring at him. "But this isn't about that. I've been doing some thinking."

She almost swayed. *I'm so tired. Please let's not do this.* "Me too."

"I think . . ." He glanced over his shoulder, at the crowd of kin. "I think you deserve to know about your mother."

"I do." She turned to Thorne, who didn't look any happier than she felt. "I . . . Thorne, will you stay? I mean, not here, you should probably go home and get some sleep, but I . . . I'd like you to, you know, hang around." *Lame, Ruby. Real lame.* But like Ell said, you had to start somewhere. "With me."

He nodded. Didn't say anything. Did he understand what she was saying? Maybe not.

She opened her mouth to try again, but he smiled. It was a sad, tired, lopsided smile, and the way he tilted his head told her he knew without her saying anything. The familiar irritation rasped again, but underneath it was deep comfort. She didn't know what to do, and that was okay. When she did, that smile said, he'd be waiting.

"Sure thing," he said, finally. "I'm not leaving here, though. My mother's on her way. She's going to rip my ears off for disappearing, but I couldn't tell her."

"When she finishes ripping your ears off, I'll do it too. Don't you *ever* do that to me again."

His smile broadened, if that was possible. "Did you miss me?"

"You're irritating. Of *course* I missed you." Ruby nodded, squared her shoulders, and turned back to Haelan.

"My mother." She folded her arms, cupping her elbows in

her hands. "Katrina. What . . . what did she do?" *Was it bad? Did she pass it down to me, do I make people taboo?*

"I . . ." He glanced at the kin, and Oncle Efraim was bearing down on them, disapproving as ever.

The tall, gaunt Oncle stopped and drew himself up. "This is clan business," he said, in his scratchy, authoritative voice. "You've been warned, Detective."

Oh sure. You won't talk to me, but you'll talk to him. Because he's got a dongle. Mithrus Christ, I am so tired of that. "Oncle Efraim." Ruby didn't even look at him. "I've asked this man a question, and I'd like to hear his answer."

What was surprising wasn't the immediate hot drift of anger and chalk-smelling dominance from Oncle Efraim. Anyone who talked to him that way, especially a kingirl, would have the same effect.

No, what was surprising was the way she sounded. Soft, polite, and completely unimpressed by his temper.

Just like Tante Rosa used to talk to him.

No, Ruby decided. She sounded like Gran.

"Your grandmother—" Efraim's voice rose, and if she didn't cut him off now, he'd become a nuisance.

"—is just down the hall, Oncle. Please keep your temper." *Now* she looked at him, and felt that same stirring inside her, dominance flexing like a muscle. "And in case you've forgotten, I'm rootfamily, and if I ask a mere-human a question, I will have an answer without interference."

Kin

The assembled kin, bright-eyed and nervous, took a collective breath.

"Now," Ruby continued, softly, inflexibly, "I think you have a family to take care of and some cleanup to organize. Those murdered girls have families too, and those families will also need their funeral costs attended to and our sincerest condolences proffered. You and Tante Sasha will attend to that personally, and Tante Sasha will have the final say in whatever decisions are made. You'd best get started."

The old man stared at her, his hands trembling. How thin was the line between him and the thing the kin had killed in Gran's garden? Control, and cruelty. Thinking you owned everything, and could do what you wanted.

Or maybe thinking you owned nothing, not even yourself, and fighting so hard to control *anything* that it made you taboo. Like a Twist, only instead of charm and badness wringing you into a corkscrew or a minotaur, you became . . . something else. Not mere-human, and not kin, either.

Oncle Efraim's trembling died down, and he nodded, slowly. The heat in his eyes faded, and his shoulders slumped. It could have been submission or relief, or both. Maybe the family gossip was wrong about what had happened in his house.

Maybe it wasn't. But for right now, he dropped his gaze. "The Moon speaks," he murmured, the traditional reply for when a Clanmother had given her decree.

"Thorne." Ruby didn't take her gaze off Efraim. "Can you

organize a cleaning party to get over to the cottage? When Gran recovers, she won't want to come home to a shambles."

"Yes ma'am." With that slight sarcastic edge—he was still Thorne, after all—he headed for the kin in the other half of the waiting room. Which meant Oncle Efraim had to go too.

She finally looked up at the detective. He was pale, beads of sweat standing out on his forehead. "You sound just like her," he said, very softly.

"Like Gran?" *Did you hear that too?*

"Like Katy. She sometimes . . . well. She was amazing."

"What happened?" *Please tell me.*

"She . . . Your Gran wanted her to marry, to settle down. She wanted . . . other things."

"Like . . . ?"

"She was involved with someone else. Look, that part of the story isn't . . . maybe I'm wrong. Maybe you should just ask Edalie."

"I'm asking you." Where did that polite, weary but unyielding tone come from? It was just *there*.

He looked away, down the hall. When he spoke, it was just a reedy murmur. "We would talk. She'd steal away to visit me, and I knew she belonged somewhere else, but . . ." He swallowed, hard, as if the words pained him. "She came to see me. . . . It was midnight, you were sleeping. We were . . . I shouldn't be telling a little girl this."

Too late. "I have a right to know. She was *my* mother."

Did he flinch? Just a little? He ran a hand over his rust-graying hair. "Well, anyway. She was crying, shaking. Said Edalie was right. That they'd had a fight, and Edalie had threatened to do something awful. Something so bad Katy couldn't tell me."

Ruby's skin chilled.

I spoke in anger. . . . I burned it. Forgive me.

Yet Gran had, furious at Ruby's intransigence, done the same thing. *You should be collared, to save you from yourself.*

Had Gran immediately regretted it? She'd gone white, shaking, and Ruby had screamed *I hate you!* and stamped away. Afterward, Gran wanted to talk, but Ruby turned away, redirected, wouldn't listen.

I fear you may do yourself harm.

"Then . . . Ruby. You were a year old." His shoulders slumped. "She . . . Katy . . . your mother loved you. You have to know that. The last thing she said to me was that you were the only thing she never regretted. She . . . she hung herself on Courline Bridge."

That's in the core. And suicide. Another taboo, one of the biggest. No wonder the kin didn't speak her name. The Moon took those who killed themselves, kept them resting on the dark side instead of the silver face, sleeping until bit by bit, every fullmoon, a little of the madness that drove a kin to take their own life drained away. You didn't speak of them because it might disturb that quiet dreaming, and it would take longer for them to come back and try again.

Do you really believe that? Con—*Adam* would sneer.

You had to believe something. At least her mother—Katy, Katrina—hadn't done something . . . else. Something like . . . Conrad.

Adam.

Ruby swayed, straightened. "So that's what she did." *I sound really calm.* "My . . . my father. Who . . . what did he do?"

"He couldn't live without her." The detective looked very old now, and very pale. The reek of despair and alcohol on him intensified. "He was . . . weak."

"Oh." *Is he with the Moon too?* She nodded. The vast empty space inside her, a cavern of wondering, just turned out to be a tiny room.

Forgive me, Gran had pleaded, in the grip of aconite hallucinations. How often had she been up at night, running the spinning wheel, thinking about her daughter? Maybe the grief choked her, the way it did Detective Haelan. He coughed, and rubbed at the welling in his eyes.

She reached out, tentatively, and touched his hand. Fragile mere-human flesh. She slipped her fingers through his. Held on for a moment, gently. "Thank you. I never knew." The Tantes and Oncles wouldn't say anything, because it was Gran's place to speak to Ruby about it privately.

Maybe, just maybe, Gran wasn't as disappointed in her as Ruby thought.

Haelan nodded as if she'd said something profound. "I'm not sure I . . ." A deep shuddering breath. "Your father loved you too, Ruby. But he was a coward."

"I guess that's where I get it from, then." She let go, and he stared at her. "Being afraid . . . it's an awful thing. A really awful thing."

That about finished things up. He kept staring, like she was a talking fish out of the feytales.

Finally, she just turned away and started walking.

He said nothing.

Halfway down the hall to Gran's room, a thought occurred to her. She spun around, but the waiting room was abuzz with kin making plans, organizing, given a direction now. Maybe they were more comfortable with letting someone else do all the ordering around, just like she was with Ellie. God, how did Gran decide what to do?

Maybe Gran just has to decide, even when she doesn't know. She does it anyway because someone has to.

And it beggared belief, but sometimes . . . sometimes even Gran might be wrong.

Forgive me.

Your father was weak. He was a coward.

I guess that's where I get it from, then.

All she'd ever been told about her father was that he was outside the clan. Maybe . . .

He couldn't live without her.

The detective was up and walking around. Still, if you thought about it, way back behind his eyes was an emptiness. Not scary like Co—*Adam's*. No, the detective just looked sad.

Lonely.

I wonder. . . .

She shook her head. She could find him later and ask, even though she wanted to run through Trueheart Memorial's halls, catch up with him, maybe in the parking lot, maybe in a hall, and *make* him tell her something else.

Anything else.

There was something else she had to do.

FOURTY-FOUR

THE WINDOW WAS THE SAME, BUT THE TREES IN THE courtyard were edged with gray light. There was a different IV pole, and the nurse in the room—her hair was dyed red, a short cap of curls like colored straw, and it made Ruby shiver—glanced up at her. "Visiting hours aren't until—"

"This is my grandmother," Ruby told her, curtly. "Is she going to be okay?"

For a moment the older woman looked ready to tell her to get out, but then she softened, looking down at Gran's slack, sleeping face. "Dr. Roumpelstett thinks so. Once we had the toxin pinpointed, a targeted system flush administered, she started to improve very quickly. She's strong, your grandmother. Very determined."

Don't I know it. "Is she . . ." Ruby floundered, searching for a question. "Will she wake up?"

"We think so. You'd be more comfortable in the waiting room, or in the cafeteria."

Ruby was abruptly aware of how messy and wild she must look. "I belong here," she said, and that voice of calm authority maybe tipped the balance, because the nurse nodded and made a few notations on a clipboard she carried, checking the machine tracking Gran's heartbeat. It sounded strong and steady, and Gran's color was better. Her parchment hair was still sloppily braided, and maybe later Ruby would ask for a comb and fix it.

The nurse left, pulling the door almost closed. Ruby looked at the window, dawn rapidly coming up, the rain intensifying.

She peeled off her trainers, setting them neatly on the chair next to the bed. Then, carefully, so carefully, she lifted up the sheet and blankets. Slid in, degree by careful degree, working her arm under Gran's thin frame.

The old woman sighed, the way she always did when Ruby climbed into bed with her. Ruby squeezed her eyes shut, tears trickling between her lids.

One of her first real memories was Gran's breath beside her, sleeping in the big rosewood bed. Gran's stroking of her hair. *Shhh now, little kinling. All is well.*

Gran teaching her to ride a bicycle, her hand steady on the back of the seat. Gran up early to make pancakes, snapping charms to flip them on the griddle. Gran chastising her for her carelessness, Gran white-lipped when Ruby came home with scabbed knees and sap in her hair. *I expected you an hour ago. I worry, Ruby!*

How terrifying, to wonder and to worry, to see your daughter in your granddaughter's face, to be afraid of losing, to have to make all the decisions. Yet she'd always been there, holding Ruby's hand, reassuring her, protecting her, raising her.

Because Katrina was gone. Had *left*.

What if Gran, deep down . . . it was a ridiculous idea, but what if Gran was just as scared as Ruby was? What if she'd learned to cover it up, but it was still there?

Under the hospital smell, Edalie de Varre smelled faintly of her perfume, and the goodness of baking bread. Ruby snuggled in, but carefully, making sure she wasn't lying on any tubes or wires, propping Gran so that she'd be comfortable.

Finally, holding the old woman close, she sighed. Dawn strengthened in the window, and Ruby swallowed, hard.

Being scared and alone was worse than anything else, even a beast with empty eyes and scythe-claws. It was worse than the pinching, the bruising, it was worse than the certain knowledge of being a disappointment to everyone you loved.

Being scared together, though . . . that was different. It wasn't *incredibly* better, but it wasn't quite so awful. At least someone was in the boat with you, and you could make things better by comforting *them*.

"Gran?" she whispered, into Edalie's hair. "I love you. Everything's okay. Please be all right." Her throat was full, and so was her nose, but she heard Gran's heartbeat, nice and strong, under the noise from the machine. The song of her breathing, familiar as her own. "I love you so much."

Ruby de Varre shut her eyes, and finally fell asleep waiting for Gran to wake up.